THE SHADOW HORSE

By

Carl Mapps

For Pat,

Carl Mapps

This book is a work of fiction. Places, events, and situations in this story are purely fictional. Any resemblance to actual persons, living or dead, is coincidental.

ISBN: 1-4107-8174-7 (e-book)
ISBN: 1-4184-5192-4 (Paperback)

The White River National Forest, Rifle Gap State Park, Bureau of Land Management (BLM), and the state prison at Canon City, Colorado are factual

Dedication

This book is dedicated to the memory of my sister, Mary Belle, an excellent rider who always had a horse.

My only regret is that she did not live to read these stories.

I
THE SHADOW HORSE

**Published 1999 in cooperation with
The Council For Indian Education,
By Native American Publications,
Billings, Montana
Copyright 1999
Illustrations by Lloyd Mann**

Carl Mapps

Chapter 1

A PLAN

"Well, you're a sure'-nuff cowboy now," Tommy Lewis said, with a grin.

Steve Peterson had ridden Rawhide, a big buckskin gelding, the mile of dirt road to show his friend the new boots and hat he had gotten for his twelfth birthday. Tommy was a Southern Ute Indian, two years older than Steve. The two boys went to the same school down the valley, and Tommy often helped Steve and his dad when they needed a helping hand on their ranch.

Steve could hardly wait to tell Tommy about his unsuccessful search for Diamond Lil

"We know what happened to Lil!" Steve exclaimed, "Jim Novak called a couple of days ago and said he had seen a Double Diamond mare up in the forest service pasture, and she looked like she was about to foal." The little half-Arabian mare, named

Diamond Lil, had mysteriously vanished from a high mountain pasture the previous summer.

"Your dad's brand," Tommy said. "It has to be Lil. Did you get her?"

"No, we didn't," Steve said. "Dad says the wild stallion drove her out of the pasture and took her to his band of mares. He says she probably came back to her home pasture to foal, but the stud would find her and take her back."

"Yeah, that's what he does," Tommy said. "He's stolen a lot of mares out of ranch pastures. But couldn't you find her?"

"No," Steve said. "All I found was tracks. Dad had to go to a cattlemen's meeting in Glenwood that day, and he asked me if I thought I could find Lil and bring her home, so I rode old Hide up there, but Lil was gone."

"Well, if anybody could catch that mare, you could," Tommy said. "Do you think we could still find her?"

"I think she's gone again. I found tracks of a horse and some of a new foal, at the spring in that little box canyon. I'm sure it was Lil. But then I saw tracks made by a bigger, heavier horse, so I guess the stud did find her. The tracks led to an old game trail that goes up the north wall of that canyon. The trail looked kind of dangerous to me, but I was anxious to find Lil, so I rode Hide to the trail, and he went up it like he did it every day. Up on top, there wasn't a horse anywhere.

"I wonder if we'll ever find her now?" Steve said.

"Well, that's really tough," Tommy replied. "But at least we know she's alive and out there somewhere." He was silent for a couple of minutes, and then he said, "Maybe you and I could get her."

"How could we do that? A lot of ranchers have chased those horses, but no one has come near catching them."

"We wouldn't chase them."

"What, then? Trap them?"

"No," Tommy said. "My grandfather told me that an older man, who went to the Indian Peace Council on the Arkansas River in 1840 near Bent's Fort, heard the Cheyenne tell how they went out on the prairies to catch horses.

"One man went out alone, and when he found the horses, he let them see him. The horses would walk away, and the man simply stood still. He turned sideways, or turned his back to the horses, and did not look at them. Then he followed, slowly, and the process was repeated many times. He continued to follow them slowly, and when the horses stopped, with him still in sight, he would stop, then slowly walk away from the horses. The horses would take a few steps toward him. Finally, the horses would just follow the man, and he could lead them into some kind of trap. Maybe something natural, like a blind canyon, or something the Indians had made. I think it can be done."

"You mean you think it might work for two of us, or are you talking of going up there all alone to try to get Lil?" Steve asked.

5

"I'd like to try it," Tommy said. "I know that country pretty well. Dad and I hunt up there. Besides," he grinned, "you know every young Indian wants to do something to test himself. Prove to himself that he's a man."

"Can I help?" Steve asked.

"Sure. I'll need some help," Tommy replied. "We'll have to work it out." He thought for a minute, then he said, "I sure would like to catch that stallion."

"You might be able to catch Lil. She's tame," Steve said. "But the stallion? I think he's too wild."

"Maybe" Tommy agreed. "But I've thought about it a lot. Last Fall I watched him through my scope sight. That's the finest horse I've ever seen. He belongs up there, but we know the ranchers won't leave him alone. They've lost good mares, and someday they'll run him down with an airplane, or shoot him. I don't want that to happen."

"Neither do I," Steve said. Even though the stallion had stolen Lil, he did not want the horse to be killed. "Would your parents let you try to catch that stallion?"

"They might," Tommy replied. "Dad's fighting a forest fire in Idaho. It's part of his job with the Forest Service. But he calls home a lot. I'll see what Mom says about it."

Chapter 2

GETTING STARTED

Three days later, Tommy rode his horse, Blackie, to the Peterson ranch. He had a backpack tied behind the cantle of his saddle. Steve was ready to go. He didn't take a pack because Tommy would be staying alone. The two boys wasted no time getting started.

Apparently as eager as the boys to get up to the high mountain meadows, old Hide broke into his familiar, swinging trot. "Traveling Trot," Steve's dad called it. Blackie followed suit, and the boys let the horses hustle until the trail became steeper. Then, to save energy, they slowed to a walk.

When they reached the mountain meadows, the boys went to the upper end and rode into the canyon. They let their horses drink at the spring, then climbed the steep trail to the top of the canyon wall. From there, they followed an old game trail to a beaver dam and pond, about a mile from the canyon.

"I think I should camp here," Tommy said. He dismounted and took down his pack.

"Are you sure you want to stay up here all alone?" Steve asked.

"Sure," Tommy replied. "Dad and I have camped here lots of times, when we come up here hunting." He found his collapsible fishing pole and handed it to Steve. "There are rainbows in the pond," he said. "See if you can catch some while I get my camp set up. I'd like to have a couple of trout for supper, and maybe you'd like to take some home with you." In a very short time Steve had two fish for Tommy and several to take home.

"Come back a week from today," Tommy said. "If I'm not here, look for a note in the tent. If I move my camp, then look for a small duffel bag hanging on a tree limb." Steve guessed that, for Tommy, it was going to be a long week.

Up on Hide again, and with Blackie in tow, Steve started back down the trail that would take him home. *Boy,* he thought, *this is really something. Like being in an old Western movie.* Was it really happening? Looking back, Steve saw Tommy staking down his little tent in the aspen grove above the beaver pond, and wished he was staying, too.

Scouting around the next day, Tommy discovered fresh droppings and many horse tracks quite close to his camp. *Good*, he thought, *they've been grazing here.* By then it was mid-afternoon, and, satisfied, he returned to his camp at the beaver pond.

9

He found the horses early the next morning. A breeze coming his way, and plenty of tall grass and sage for concealment, made it easy to get closer to the band of horses. Then, without showing himself, Tommy sat behind a bush and began playing a wooden flute. His grandfather had made it a long time ago, from two pieces of cedar glued together and bound with rawhide. He played the flute for a little while, then he began singing a soft, sing-song chant.

Hearing him, the horses raised their heads and looked his way. In a few minutes they resumed their grazing.

Again, Tommy alternated playing the flute and singing, until the horses paid no more attention to the sound. Then, slowly, he stood up and showed himself, keeping his back to the horses. He knew that if he faced the horses, and made eye contact, he would appear threatening.

The horses moved away, but they did not run. Tommy remained quietly standing while he played the flute again. The horses did not go far, and they soon went back to grazing. Tommy took just a few steps toward the horses, still not looking directly at them, and again the horses moved away.

Very deliberately, showing no sign of haste, Tommy repeated the procedure, over and over. He spent that day gradually working his way closer to the band, and began the same thing the next day.

Most of the horses were branded mares. Coming from ranches, they were used to people and were a calming influence on the band. The big stallion kept his distance, always staying on the far side of the herd from where Tommy was, but he did not run off. By the end of the second day, Tommy was able to get near some of the mares and even pet them. Always, he talked quietly, and sometimes played the flute. The horses were beginning to accept his presence.

Diamond Lil, still protective of her foal, was shy, but finally she allowed Tommy to approach, and then to pet her. He pulled a handful of tall grass to use as a grooming tool, and soon Lil enjoyed being brushed.

Tommy liked, most of all, watching the stallion at play. The young colts kicked up their heels and dashed about, having pretend battles. Sometimes they charged the stallion, made believe they were attacking him, then raced away. The big stallion would join the play, and then he circled the band at a furious pace, apparently running for the sheer joy of it. Often he reared, stood almost straight up, and pawed the air with his front feet. The proud animal seemed to be informing all the world that he was bigger, stronger, faster, and in every way superior to any other horse. He was the king of the hill.

The stallion was a deep mahogany bay, with black lower legs, mane, and tail. As though aware of his ability to blend with the scenery, the stallion frequently dashed into a thicket, or the shade of a stand of trees, where he simply disappeared. "No wonder they call you the shadow horse," Tommy told the big bay horse. "That's a good name for you all right. The Shadow Horse." Tommy enjoyed talking to horses. He felt that it brought them closer together.

Chapter 3

CATCHING LIL

The week seemed to have ended very quickly, and yet Tommy knew that he was as ready as he ever would be. Would his scheme work? If there was a commotion and the horses ran off, could he hold Lil? He dare not let her get away wearing a halter and dragging a rope. She could get hung up on something, and probably would. Unable to graze or get to water, she would die very soon.

In spite of his worries, Tommy felt that he had a good chance of accomplishing what he had set out to do.

Steve found a note in the tent. It said,
Tie the horses out of sight and wait
for me. I'm coming with Lil. Tommy.

I wonder why he wants me to wait here? Steve wondered, as he tied Hide and Blackie back in the trees. *Well, if that's what he wants me to do, I'd better do it. I'll just go out a little way and watch for him.*

When Tommy had haltered Diamond Lil and began working her out of the band, he was pleased to see that the foal stayed close. The wary stallion would quickly detect any excitement, even nervousness, among the horses in the band. Much as he wanted to, Tommy neither hurried nor looked back. Instead, he watched the other mares for any abnormal reaction.

"Good girl," Tommy spoke to Lil. He wanted to hold her attention and delay the moment when she realized she was being led away from the other horses. Then he was in the clear, moving away from the band. *Good*, he thought. *It's working.* And then, with no warning, Lil raised her head and whinnied.

Every horse looked up. For a moment, the stallion stood motionless. Then he neighed shrilly and charged through the band, scattering horses in every direction. Instinctively, Tommy tugged Lil to a tree and quickly wrapped the lead rope around it. He grabbed his pocket knife and held it ready to cut Lil's halter if he had to release her. He would never be able to unbuckle it in all the commotion. Her foal stayed close against her.

The rapidly approaching stallion was a fearsome sight. Tommy was certain he would have to let Lil go to save himself from being trampled. Determined to wait until the last possible second, he held his knife ready. And then, when he was only a few feet away, the charging horse abruptly slid to a stop, spun around, and galloped after the mares, all quickly disappearing.

Trembling from fear and excitement, Tommy looked back to see what had stopped the stallion. It was Steve, running toward him, waving his arms and yelling.

For a few minutes, both boys were breathless and unable to speak. When he found his voice, Steve said, "I found the note. I guess I should have waited like you said, but I wanted to come out and meet you. When I saw that stallion coming, I thought he would run right over you. Maybe I shouldn't have come out. Did I cause all that trouble."

"You saved the day, is what you did. And maybe my life, too," Tommy laughed. "I don't know what would have happened if you hadn't come running. Lil would be gone again, for sure." While they trudged to the camp at the beaver pond, Tommy told Steve how he had gotten Lil out of the band.

"Boy, this is something!" Steve exclaimed. "We've got Lil and her foal."

"Yes, but they're not home yet," Tommy said. "Let's pack up and get down to the ranch."

Chapter 4

STEVE'S SURPRISE

"Well, Tommy," Orlo Peterson said, "you proved that there really is more than one way to skin a cat." Tommy and the Petersons watched Diamond Lil eat hay while her foal explored the confines of the corral. "I don't know how I can repay you," he added.

"I'm just glad that it worked out," Tommy said. "I wanted to give it a try. And I think we were lucky."

"Maybe so," Orlo replied. "But you got it done. And you're right about that stallion. This is a fine looking colt. What are you going to name him, Steve?"

"You want me to name him?"

"Well, sure. If you two hadn't cooked up a plan, we wouldn't have Lil, would we? The colt's yours, if you want him."

Steve's grin lit up the ranch. "Tommy says the colt will shed out to be a golden chestnut, like his mother," he said. "Maybe I'll call him Nugget."

15

"Good name," Orlo replied. Then he said, "I wish we could let this pair run in the forest service pasture this summer. There's no better way to grow strong, healthy colts. And good feet. But as long as that stud is out there, we can't do it."

"Tommy wants to try to get the stallion," Steve said.

"I understand how you feel about that, Tommy," Orlo said. "He's a fine horse, and we'd all like to see him caught. But maybe he's too wild. Well, let's get hold of Nugget. It's a good time to start his education."

Chapter 5

BACK IN THE WILD COUNTRY

"That horse might be dangerous," Steve said, as the two friends again rode the mountain trail to the beaver pond. Orlo Peterson had met with some of the ranchers, and they had agreed to give Tommy until Labor Day to try to catch the stallion.

"I know," Tommy said. "He might be dangerous, and untamable. But we have two-and-a-half weeks, and I would hate to think that I didn't even try to get that stallion."

This time, both boys carried packs on their horses. When they got to the beaver pond and unloaded the horses, Tommy dug out his fishing tackle, and they put a couple of flies on the water. While they fished, Tommy went over the plan with Steve.

"Give me another week," he said. "Then come back and see how I'm doing. We'll follow the same plan if I have to move."

Steve wondered, for the second time that summer, if they were doing the right thing. *Were they being foolish? Getting Lil was one thing,* he thought. *But the stallion?* He shivered when he recalled seeing the furiously charging horse.

When he returned a week later, Steve found a note that said,

> I'm going to move my camp to the
> south side of Big Baldy Mountain.
> Don't go there unless I tell you to.
> Look for another note in the bag
> hung from the tree branch. Things
> are going okay so far. Tommy.

Steve had brought beef jerky, canned bacon, powdered eggs, dried milk, candy bars, apples, and a small sack of horse pellets. He put it all in the duffel bag and hung it as high as he could on a stout branch. Wild animals would smell the food, especially the apples and pellets. Then he left his own note, climbed into his saddle, and sat for a few minutes, looking wistfully over at Big Baldy Mountin.

Tommy had worked his way into the broodmare band almost as though nothing had happened. But the stallion seemed more wary than before, always moving away from Tommy. *Would that wild horse ever let him come near?* Tommy hoped he would not have to resort to a tranquilizer fired from a rifle.

His grandfather had told how the plains Indians sometimes ran wild horses down by jogging along after them day after day, not allowing them to eat or drink. In a few days, men could get close enough to the weakened animals to rope those they wanted, or perhaps drive them into a trap. He thought about what a tremendous amount of endurance that would take.

Tommy did not intend to do that. He did not like the idea, and he knew, also, that in the mountains there was grass right under foot and water everywhere. To say nothing of the many, many good places for a horse to hide.

He realized that, although catching Diamond Lil had been relatively easy, getting the shadow horse was another matter entirely. Maybe even impossible. He felt that eventually he could get a rope on the stallion, but did he have enough time? It was almost Labor Day.

When he went back to the beaver pond to move his camp, Tommy grinned when he found what Steve had left for him. The apples were going to be a real treat. And the horse pellets. *Why didn't I think of that?* he asked himself. *Steve,* he thought, *you might be helping more than you realize.* His spirits were improved considerably.

But the next morning, like the proverbial bolt from the blue, disaster struck.

Carl Mapps

Chapter 6

TROUBLE COMES A'RUNNING

Tommy was with Old Bess, as he had named one of the gentle mares. She had a filly, probably about four months old, at her side, and Tommy was trying to coax the filly to eat an apple core when suddenly every horse raised its head and stood perfectly still, listening.

Then he heard a galloping horse, and a moment later saw a horse and rider, coming fast. In a flash, the big stallion circled the band, bunching them and driving them away from the oncoming horseman. Having fled from danger many times, the horses took off in a wild rush.

Without even thinking about it, when Old Bess turned to run Tommy grabbed a handful of mane and swung onto the mare's back. Leaning over her neck, he clutched the thick mane and gripped with his legs. Looking up, he was horrified to see all the horses going full speed right over the edge of a bluff. Then he looked back and saw the horseman aiming a gun at the stallion. The last thing Tommy saw before Old Bess plunged over the rim of the bluff was the stallion lunging at the charging horse. And he thought he heard a rifle shot.

Plunging down the slope, Old Bess kept her feet under her until the stallion and the other horse, riderless now, came tumbling down and crashed into her. Tommy went flying, hit the ground rolling, slammed into something, and blacked out.

All was still, strangely so, when Tommy regained consciousness. He could hear nothing but the peaceful snuffling and foot stomping of grazing horses. Curious, he sat up, and the world began to spin. He lay back down for a moment, then, carefully, he sat up again. Much to his surprise, the band of mares, apparently none the worse for their mad dash over the bluff, grazed calmly, as though nothing unusual had happened.

Okay. Good, he thought. But where was the stallion? Then he saw, near the bottom of the slope, the stallion and a saddled horse, lying a few yards apart. Were they dead?

Fearful, weak, and shaking, Tommy ignored aches and pains, struggled to his feet, and went to the stallion. The big horse was breathing, but he did not look good. Cautiously, Tommy examined the horse's legs and found that apparently there were no broken bones. The other horse was also alive, but one foreleg was unnaturally twisted. Tommy knew it was broken.

"This is bad. Real bad," Tommy muttered. Bad enough, and he had not even found the man who had ridden the horse. He was not sure that he even wanted to find that man, but he scanned the slope and, higher up, he located the man lodged against a tree. That didn't look good either. Not good at all.

Tommy struggled up to where the injured man lay and found that he was breathing, and moaning faintly. *Alive, thank the Lord*, Tommy mused. He knew it was considered wrong to move an injured person, but help was miles away, so he decided it would be better to move the man than to leave him wrapped awkwardly around the tree. The man was big. Real big, and it took all the strength Tommy could muster to get the injured man away from the tree and into a more natural position. In doing so, he discovered the man's right leg was broken below the knee.

"Wonderful. Just wonderful," Tommy muttered as he plodded up the bluff to get to his camp. What else could go wrong?

He noticed that his strength gradually returned as he walked to camp. But not his confidence. The situation looked pretty bad. Thus far in his life, Tommy had never been confronted with anything as serious as what he faced here. And the grim reality was that there was nobody else around to help, or to advise him. Or maybe there was.

As he dragged his camping gear down to the bottom of the bluff, Tommy tried to imagine what his dad would say. *Don't lose your head,* for one thing. And, *Heck, you can do it. Just take it one step at a time, and do the best you can*. Those thoughts helped considerably. And yet, Tommy could not shake the notion of personal responsibility that lurked in the back of his mind. Had he made a big mistake, he wondered, coming out here, chasing a wild horse?

He would try to splint the broken leg before the man woke up. *And,* he wondered, *what if he doesn't wake up?* "Don't even think about it," he told himself.

Tommy hesitated momentarily before grabbing the booted foot and pulling the broken leg straight. Then he gritted his teeth and pulled harder. There was a little jolt, like something slipped, and the leg looked better. The big man moaned but did not wake up.

Tommy padded the leg with a folded blanket, placed two fairly stout sticks on opposite sides of the leg, and bound the whole thing with a piece of rope. Then, using a blanket for a sled, he dragged the man down to the bottom of the slope and covered him with yet another blanket. His last one. He was out of blankets, but still had his sleeping bag.

I need to find that rifle, Tommy thought. He had to hunt for a while, but he found the gun, and was pleased to see it appeared to be undamaged. The action worked, and there were cartridges in the magazine.

Not liking it at all, Tommy went to the saddled horse, and took another look at its twisted broken leg. Then he aimed the rifle at a spot exactly between and just above the horse's eyes, and pulled the trigger. Knowing that the horse died instantly and painlessly didn't help much. Tommy had never had to do that before, and it made him feel a little bit sick. But he was glad that it was over. "We do a lot of things we don't like to do," his father had told him. *Dad's a good teacher,* Tommy thought. *He said you never know what's going to happen; life's full of surprises. And he sure was right about that.*

Then, finally, he went to the stallion. The horse was breathing easier, and his ears moved when Tommy stepped close. *I had better hurry*, he thought. The big horse was reviving, and if that strong animal got to his feet he would certainly run off. Or try to.

Tommy hurried down to his pack, grabbed a denim jacket, two pair of hobbles, a halter, and his lariat.

He used the jacket for a blindfold, then fit the halter over it. Working carefully, knowing that, even blindfolded, if the horse woke up it could strike out at him with its powerful legs, he hobbled the front and hind feet. He tied one end of the lariat to a rear hobble, ran it through a front hobble, and tied a quick-release knot, so that movement of the legs and feet was possible but somewhat restricted. He wished he could stay with the horse, but he still had much to do.

Chapter 7

TOMMY'S BUSY DAY

Moaning and groaning, the injured man slowly regained consciousness. He raised his head, looked all around, and fixed his eyes on Tommy.

"What happened?" he asked.

"We had a wreck. You had a bad fall and your leg's broken." Tommy helped the man sit up, and gave him some water.

"Are you the Indian who was going to catch that wild stallion?"

"Yes. That's what I wanted to do."

"I shot him," the big man growled. "Is he dead?"

"No, he's not dead. You might have missed him," Tommy replied. "He's hurt, though," he went on. Pointing, he said, "That's him, lying up there."

"Well," the grounded man asserted, "I'll sure finish him, soon's I find my rifle. Know where it is?"

"Here it is," Tommy said. "Your horse had a broken leg, and I had to shoot him."

"All right, let's have it. I'll finish the job."

Tommy grinned and said, "Well, here's your gun, but you're not going to shoot the horse." He watched the man's puzzled look, and said, "I've got all the ammunition."

The injured man began to cuss, and then he couldn't help smiling. He admired a nervy kid.

"I'm Joe Morgan," he said. "Call me Joe."

"I'm Tommy Lewis." Tommy held out his hand.

"Al Lewis's boy?" Tommy nodded as they shook hands. "I know Al. Smoke jumper, ain't he?"

"Yes, that's him," Tommy replied. Then he asked, "How do you feel?"

"I don't know. I guess my leg's all that's broken. But I've got a terrible headache."

"I'll get a fire going and make some coffee," Tommy said. "Then I'll get a camp set up and fix something to eat."

"There's a thermos of coffee and some sandwiches in my saddlebags, if they're not all smashed."

The stainless steel thermos was undamaged. The sandwiches seemed to be kind of mashed, but they might still be edible. He took those items down to Morgan and began to get his camp organized. Then he inquired, "How're you doing?"

"Okay, considering. Better, now that I've had some coffee. It could be worse. You're doin' a good job, kid. I'm glad one of us is still able to get around."

Tommy had a bowl of soup and ate some bread and peanut butter, then helped Morgan get in the little tent. That done, he filled a canvas camp bucket with water from the stream flowing through the mountain meadow and went to the stallion.

He loosened the quick-release knot on the long rope, then went to the front and, pulling on the halter rope, lifted the horse's head and encouraged him to get up. The weakened stallion tried, then lay back down. Tommy let him rest for a few minutes, then repeated the process. This time the horse struggled to his feet and stood, swaying and trembling. Tommy held the bucket of water to his muzzle. The big horse sniffed, snorted, sniffed again, and drank the bucket dry.

He took several deep breaths, shook himself, and tried to walk. Finding his feet hobbled, he struggled, and Tommy had to stop him. He used the lariat to take up slack as the horse shuffled, and when all four feet were bunched, Tommy grasped the horse's tail and pulled sideways. Unable to balance himself, the stallion went down. The fall was uphill, as Tommy had planned, which made it easier on the horse. Tommy hurried back to the stream with the bucket, while the exhausted horse lay resting.

Not wanting the big horse to lie down any longer than necessary, with his breathing and circulation restricted, Tommy again urged him to stand. Again, the horse got to his feet, and then Tommy discovered the bullet wound. There was a long, ugly gash on the off, or right shoulder, hard to see because of all the dirt and grass covering it. The horse had been lying on it.

"Well, old horse, we're going to have to take care of that," Tommy said. He put a hand on the horse's neck and tried to work down to the shoulder, but the frightened animal again struggled to escape; Tommy had to lay him down again, to prevent the determined horse from further injuring himself. "I hate to do that," he told the horse, "but there's no other way." The wound had to be cleaned and treated. If the stallion ran off in his present condition, he would very likely die of infection.

Tommy stayed with the horse all through that night, and had to lay him down several times. While the horse was down, Tommy quietly ran his hands over the horse's body, and gradually the stallion began to tolerate being touched. Tommy had to show the horse that it had nothing to fear, that it could trust him, and he thought he was making progress with that. From time to time, Tommy blew gently at the horse's nostrils, so it always would know him.

By daylight, the stallion had stopped trying to run off, and, for the first time, Tommy left him standing while he went to the tent to check on Morgan. He found the man still snoring, so went to the meadow and pulled an armful of the lush grass. After some hesitation the wary horse nibbled, then eagerly ate the grass, and seemed to calm down as Tommy stroked his neck. He talked quietly whenever he was with the horse. Pleased with the way Shadow, as he began calling the stallion, was responding, Tommy wished he had some kind of medication for the ugly bullet wound. He went back to the meadow for more grass, and brought another bucket of water when he went back to the stallion. By then, the horse was tolerating being touched over most of his body, and Tommy was able, being careful and taking lots of time, to clean the wound. Fortunately, as it turned out, Tommy's mother had insisted on his putting a bar of soap in his pack, and now Tommy grinned when he thought how little of it he had used.

"Well, horse," he said, "it's coming in handy after all, isn't it? I wish we had some disinfectant, but we don't, and I guess this will get us by."

Chapter 8

AN INDIAN TRICK

The smell of perking coffee and frying bacon greeted Morgan when he woke up. He slid himself out of the tent and sat up.

"How are you feeling?" Tommy asked.

"My leg aches, but I guess I'm okay otherwise," Morgan said. "I'm hungry, so I guess I'm all right."

"I'm glad to hear that," Tommy said. He brought Morgan coffee, scrambled eggs, bacon, and flapjacks.

"You're fulla surprises," Morgan smiled. Then he asked, "Are we gonna get some help up here?"

"Yes, I'm going to try to see to that," Tommy replied. He didn't elaborate. Morgan would think him foolish.

When he had eaten, Tommy pulled another armful of grass and took it to the stallion. "I'm going to leave you for a while," he told the horse. "So don't

31

throw a fit and hurt yourself." He stopped at his camp and picked up the blanket Morgan had been using. Then he went up the slope.

Up there, he cleared ground to make a good-sized fireplace and got a fire burning. Then, using his small camp ax, he began cutting branches from pine trees. When the fire was burning strong enough, he added the green wood and went to cut more. Carrying an armful of fuel to the fire, he was pleased to see a plume of black smoke going high in the still morning air. *Perfect*, he thought.

He held the blanket spread out above the fire for a moment to cut off the smoke, then he raised one side to let a big puff of smoke out. He did this several times. *I don't know the signals my ancestors used*, he thought, *but if someone's looking at the smoke this'll tell them it's a signal, not just a fire.*

Tommy cut more fuel, then he pulled an armful of the more nutritious upland grass and went down to Shadow. The stallion munched the grass and nudged Tommy with his nose.

"I thought you'd like that," Tommy said, as he stroked the horse's back. He was satisfied with the progress he had made, but he knew that one wrong move doubtless would panic the barely tamed horse. With time running out, he would be back to square one.

"You think you're going to take that horse home?" Morgan asked, when Tommy went back to the campsite.

"I hope so," Tommy replied.

"You're a wishful thinker. I don't think you'll ever tame that horse. He'll get away again, some day."

"I think it's worth a try," Tommy said. "That stallion has good blood in him. Look at those yearlings."

"Yeah, they do look good, but maybe they'll have too much wild in them," Morgan said. Then he asked, "Say, are we going to get some help up here?"

"I hope so. Look up there." Tommy pointed to the column of smoke above the bluff.

"Yeah, I saw that. Looks like somebody's got a fire. But I couldn't figure out the puff of smoke I saw few minutes ago."

"Smoke signal." Tommy grinned. "Steve Peterson is keeping an eye out, and my dad, too, if he's home. If they see the smoke, they'll know I need help."

"I'll be darned," Morgan said, surprised. "An old Indian trick. Well, if nothing else, the fire lookout'll probably see it. I hope it works."

"If nobody comes today, I'll ride out tomorrow."

"You'll ride out!" Morgan exclaimed. "On what, your wild stud?"

"I'll show you," Tommy replied with a smile. He picked up a short piece of rope and went down to the mares. He found Old Bess, looped the rope and fashioned a halter. Then he grabbed a handful of mane and swung onto the mare's back. With only the halter, he rode Bess at a walk, then a trot. The mare obediently circled both ways, then stopped when asked.

33

"A lot of these mares are ranch raised and tamed," Tommy said when he came back to the campsite. "I might even ask to borrow your saddle, if I can get it off that dead horse."

"Looks like that might work," Morgan said.

"Yes," Tommy replied, and went on, "and it seems to me that it will be pretty easy to come out here and get all those mares, if I can get the stallion home."

"That's a pretty big 'if'."

"We'll see," Tommy said. "You can help yourself to the coffee. I have to get busy."

He went up to the signal fire and added more green wood, then he went down to the stallion, now standing quietly. He had pellets in his pocket, and after a bit of investigative sniffing, the big horse ate one, and looked for more. Then Tommy began the slow progress of coaxing the stallion ahead, a step at a time, using the pellets for bait. He knew that suggestion, with a reward for every right response, would accomplish what force would not.

Down in the meadow, finally, Tommy stroked the stallion's neck and said, "Well, Shadow, you know how to move with the hobbles. Now you can feed yourself, and get a drink when you want one."

"You're doing pretty good with that horse," Morgan said, when Tommy came back to the campsite. "But," he went on, "I think that the minute you take the blindfold off he'll be gone, hobbles and all."

"Maybe," Tommy said. "But he learns fast, and doesn't seem to fear me any more."

Morgan smiled, but he said nothing.

Chapter 9

HELP ARRIVES

Tommy went back up to the top of the bluff to put out the signal fire. Although foliage was still green and there seemed to be little danger of fire spreading, he dare not take that chance. He was stomping out hot coals when he heard the thrum of trotting horses.

Three riders came into view, and Tommy recognized Steve and Orlo Peterson, and his own dad, Al Lewis. Steve saw Tommy and urged Hide to a gallop.

"Hey, Tommy, what's happening?" he asked when he got closer.

"Everything that could happen, did happen," Tommy said. And added, "You probably won't believe it when I tell you." By then, Al and Orlo had ridden up, and Tommy explained, briefly, what had occurred.

"I know Joe Morgan," Orlo said. "He wasn't at the meeting we had, about giving you until Labor Day to try to catch the stallion. He didn't know about that."

"I'll try to get somebody on the radio," Al said. "We can get a forest service chopper up here, but I think they'll wait till morning to come. It's going to be dark real soon."

"Let's get unpacked," Orlo suggested. "We don't want to take these geldings down there, where the stallion is. Might cause trouble. We'll sleep up here, where we can keep an eye on thc horses."

"Good idea," Al said. They unsaddled, hobbled their horses, and then went down the slope to Tommy's campsite.

"Hello, Joe," Orlo said to Morgan. "How're you doing?"

"Well, I've been better," Morgan replied. "But I'm pretty good, considering. You've got a good boy there, Al."

"I'm glad to hear that," Al said. "We'll have a chopper here first thing in the morning."

Tommy stirred up the cooking fire, and then Orlo and Al began fixing supper.

"Let's go see the stallion, Steve," Tommy suggested, and they went down to the horses.

"The apples and pellets were a great idea," Tommy said. "And the extra food, too. I hadn't expected company." He fussed with the stallion while the big horse investigated Steve. "They called him the shadow horse," Tommy said, "and I've named him Shadow."

Back at the campfire, Al said to Tommy, "It looks like your plans got changed. But you've got the stallion. Do you think you can get him home?"

"I hope so. I'm going to try, anyway," Tommy said. Then he went on, "But for right now, I think I'll get some sleep." With a big lot of worry lifted from his shoulders, Tommy suddenly realized how tired he was.

Chapter 10

GOING HOME

Early the next morning Tommy and Al Lewis, along with Steve and Orlo Peterson, watched the disappearing helicopter.

"Well, Joe's on his way!" Al said. "And we'd better be going, too."

He and Orlo were to go on ahead. They had pulled Morgan's saddle from the dead horse, and Tommy fitted it to Old Bess. She would carry the camping gear, and she and her foal would accompany Steve and Tommy as they brought the stallion out.

"You boys be careful," Orlo said. "Let that horse go if you have to, but don't get yourself hurt."

"Yes," Al agreed, "your safety is more important than the horse. Okay?" Tommy and Steve agreed to that, and then Al and Orlo climbed into their saddles and, with Rawhide in tow, started for home.

Working carefully, trying to stay as far out of reach of the horse's feet as possible, Tommy fastened a rope around the stallion's girth, to make a crude surcingle. Then he unbuckled the hobble from Shadow's left foreleg and tied one end of the long rope to that leg. He passed that long rope through the surcingle, under the horse's belly. From there, he ran it through a loop on the still-attached right foreleg hobble. With that done, he carefully removed the hobbles from the stallion's hind legs.

"There," Tommy said, "that's a makeshift 'running W'. He's free to walk, but if he tries to run, we should be able to pull his front feet out from under him. I might need your help with that. Now, we have to hope that what training he's had to lead will be enough, but this is something different."

Tommy tried to lead the stallion, but Shadow shook his head, pulled back, and even tried to rear up till Tommy pulled him down. Never having had a halter on before, or been controlled by a man, the horse struggled against the force of the rope.

Tommy worked patiently with Shadow, talking to him, calming him down. In a few minutes, Tommy had the horse moving, although somewhat unwillingly, in his direction.

Finally, Tommy said to Steve, "Okay, you go ahead with Bess. Take it real slow going up the bluff."

Getting up the steep slope was no problem for Old Bess and her foal, although, with the blindfold, it was enough of a struggle for Shadow so that he quit fighting the lead rope and concentrated on getting up the rocky slope.

Once on top, even though he was still blindfolded, Shadow made an attempt to run away. Watching for that, Tommy was quick enough to dig in his heels and sit back on the rope and bring the stallion to his knees. There were no more escape attempts.

It was a couple of miles to the beaver pond, and the boys stopped several times, during which Tommy let the stallion graze, and he talked to the horse, petted him, and kept Bess close for reassuring company. Once at the pond, Tommy suggested staying there for the night. "I think this is enough for one day, for Shadow," Tommy said. "And I don't want to try to go down that steep trail on the canyon wall in the dark. We'll do it in the morning."

Steve agreed with that, and unpacked and unsaddled Bess, then hobbled her. Tommy replaced Shadow's hobbles, front and rear, then removed the surcingle and the "W" rig. Both horses were groomed, then turned loose to graze.

"When will you take the blindfold off?" Steve asked.

"Not until I have him home, and in the corral," Tommy answered. Then he said, "We've got him this far, and I don't want to take any chances."

Steve grinned, and said, "It's hard to believe that you've got the wild stallion. That's really something."

"It will be, if our luck holds," Tommy agreed. Then he said, "Let's get a couple of trout for supper." That night, more relaxed than they had been for a while, the two boys slept soundly under the stars, in the beautiful, clear weather.

The next morning, while they ate breakfast, Steve said, "It's so nice up here, I hate to leave."

"We'll be back," Tommy said. "You'll be riding Diamond Lil and I'll be riding the shadow horse." Grinning, he held his crossed fingers aloft.

Packed up and started for home, each privately wondered how Shadow would manage the treacherous trail going down the canyon wall. Unsure how it would work, Tommy had one idea. When they came to where the trail started down, he stepped in front of the horse and took a short hold on the lead rope. When he felt the steeply descending path, Shadow put his nose against Tommy's back for guidance and went down the steep trail without missing a step.

"That's a smart horse," Steve commented.

"Yes, but he lived in these mountains, and he knows this trail. I'll bet he knows right where he is."

"Yeah, maybe," Steve agreed. They led their horses down to the spring and let them drink before beginning the final leg of the homeward journey.

Chapter 11

SHADOW'S NEW HOME

The next morning Tommy was in the corral, applying salve to the already-healing bullet wound on Shadow's shoulder. Steve was carefully brushing the stallion's sleek hide.

"It's hard to believe you did it," Al Lewis said. "This is something you will never forget. Neither will any of us." Then he asked, "When are you going to take the blindfold off?"

"How about right now?"

"Yeah," Al said, "you have to do it sometime." Everyone moved quickly out of the corral and left Tommy alone with the big stallion.

Tommy hesitantly loosened the blindfold. Then, while talking to the horse and stroking his neck with one hand, Tommy slowly let in a little light and then, still talking and rubbing the horse's neck, he took the blindfold completely off.

The stallion raised his head, blinked his eyes, and looked around. "Easy, boy, easy," Tommy said. Seeing the horse tensing his muscles and rolling his eyes, Tommy quickly unsnapped the lead rope from Shadow's halter and stepped back. Shadow still wore hobbles on his front feet, but he had learned to move with them on, and move he did.

Lunging powerfully, the big stallion dashed to the corral fence, then turned and circled the whole corral, hopping as best he could. In a few minutes, the big horse began to settle down, and Tommy began talking to him again. The horse stopped, finally, and, hearing Tommy's familiar voice, he looked toward the sound. Very carefully, Tommy eased through the corral gate. Talking to the horse, and trying not to show fear or excitement, he very slowly approached the trembling horse. Those watching from outside the corral didn't even breathe.

"Easy, boy, easy. Good boy; that's good," Tommy said, while, one step at a time, he came closer to the horse. When he was close enough, Tommy reached out one hand, slowly, and held it. The stallion lowered his head, sniffed the hand, and began to relax. Still talking soothingly to the horse, Tommy moved a bit closer, so that he could, with his fingers, begin rubbing Shadow's muzzle, then up between the eyes. The horse accepted Tommy's touch, and so, still being cautious, Tommy moved closer and finally began stroking Shadow's neck.

The big horse relaxed even more, and yet Tommy spent quite a long time petting the horse before he snapped the lead rope to the halter. Then, very gently, he asked the stallion to step forward, and, surprisingly, the horse followed Tommy over to the manger to stand beside Old Bess. Again, Tommy unsnapped the lead rope, and, without hurrying, he walked across the corral and out the gate.

"I think you took a chance there, Tommy," his dad said.

"Yeah, maybe I did," Tommy replied. "I thought he might run from me, but I didn't think he would try to hurt me. I kind of trusted him, and I guess he trusted me. But I think it's real good that we have Old Bess here to keep him company."

* * * * * * * * *

Two days later, Tommy had just gotten off the school bus and entered the corral, when a pickup truck drove into the yard. The door on the passenger side opened and Joe Morgan climbed out. He wore a walking cast and carried a pair of stout crutches.

"Hello, Mr. Morgan," Tommy said, as he came out of the corral. "How are you?"

"Oh, I'm fine. You should go to medical school. The doctor said my leg is good just the way you fixed it. Is your dad around?"

"Yes. Here he comes."

Al had heard the pickup's arrival, and he was stepping out the back door of the house.

Morgan turned and said, "Hello, Al. I wanted to see Tommy and his horse. That boy's fulla surprises, ain't he?"

"I guess maybe he is," Al replied, and said, "I'm glad to see you're okay."

"I am, thanks to that boy of yours. I want to say to both of you that I'm sorry about what happened. I'd have been in a real bad fix if Tommy hadn't been there. Looks like I got a little reckless."

"Thanks, Joe. We appreciate your coming."

Morgan turned back to Tommy then, and said, "I'm glad to see that stallion in a pen, finally. Do you think that corral will hold him?"

"It needs some more fixing," Tommy said. "We're working on it."

"Good. Well, the horse does seem to be right at home here."

"Old Bess is company for him," Tommy said. "But she's branded. The JN is Jim Novak's brand. He'll want to take her home."

"Let me know if he does," Morgan said. "I can bring one of my mares. The horse won't want to be alone. And we ought to try to get the rest of those horses before winter. Can you help us with that, Tommy?"

"Sure. I want to do that," Tommy said. "Steve will want to help, and probably his dad, too.

"Good. Real good."

* * * * * * * * *

A few days later Joe Morgan, Jim Novak, Orlo Peterson, and two other ranchers showed up at the Lewis ranch. Morgan's pickup pulled a trailer loaded with baled hay. They found Al Lewis working at the corral.

"Mornin', Al," Morgan said. "I brought you some hay."

"That's not necessary, not at all," Al objected.

"I think it is. You don't have much time, or enough land, to put up hay. Too late for that, anyway. We've got an idea."

"Oh? What's up?"

"Some of us will want mares bred to that stallion," Morgan began. "But he's a wild horse, or has been. We don't want him to get loose again. Well, to cut it short, the horse needs a real good pen. Some of us would like to get together and build him one. Make it bigger, with a shed and all. It ought to be here. After all, it's Tommy's horse."

"Here?" Al was surprised. "That's a generous offer. I don't know, we'll have to think about that for a while. This is more than we would expect."

* * * * * * * * *

One week later a caravan of trucks and trailers, stirring up a cloud of dust on the dirt road, pulled into the Lewis ranch. Men unloaded tools and materials and went to work. After marking out the area, two men with a power auger started drilling post-holes. A couple of men followed and set posts, and the rest of the men strung the woven wire that was made especially for horses. They finished that day, and returned the next to build a shed, complete with a feed room and manger. Al said he would run a water line and put in a tank.

Chapter 12

THE STUDENT TEACHER

"Are you going to try to break that horse to ride?" Al Lewis leaned on the gate, watching Tommy pick up droppings in the pen.

"I sure would like to be able to ride him," Tommy replied.

"I don't blame you," Al said. "But that worries me. This is no ordinary horse."

"I've thought about that, too," Tommy said. "But I have a lot of confidence in that horse. He's already quite tame. He leads fine, and he's hobble broke. It's a good start."

"Yes," Al said, "all of that is true. But I have to wonder if we have the experience to train him. He's no two-year-old colt. You can't snub him up to another saddle horse. He's too big and strong. It would be dangerous for the snubbing horse and for both riders."

"I know," Tommy agreed. "What I would like to do, is just to start working with Shadow, be real careful, and see how he does. I'll have to watch him, and try to figure it out as I go along."

"Well, okay. But I'm going to be gone again. Don't ever forget that this is a wild horse. He's tremendously strong, and quick, and he can kill a man, or another horse, in the blink of an eye."

"I won't forget that," Tommy assured his dad.

* * * * * * * * * *

"Come on, Shadow," Tommy said. He led the horse to a fence post. "We have things to do, and the first thing you have to do is learn to stand tied." He passed the halter shank twice around the fence post and held the rest of the rope in his hand.

"We won't tie it yet, though," he continued talking to the horse. "Too many horses have been ruined that way." As he talked, he ran his free hand over Shadow's neck, then the shoulder, and then down the leg. He had brought the hobbles with him, and he buckled them on. If was a safety precaution – just in case.

Tommy had brought out an old saddle blanket, and now, with his free hand, he let Shadow sniff it, and look at it, and then he began rubbing the blanket on Shadow's back. Those times, back on Old Baldy Mountain, when Tommy had to throw Shadow and tie him down, made it easier now to accustom the horse to having the blanket moved all around his body and down the legs.

The next day Tommy tied Shadow, but with a quick-release knot. He flapped the saddle blanket all around without spooking the horse, and then he brought out his saddle. Again, Shadow sniffed, and looked at this new object. But it smelled like horses, and sweat, and like all old leather does, and those were familiar smells by now. Shadow fidgeted some, but accepted the saddle without too much fuss. Tommy left it on the horse's back for a few minutes, then took it off, and put it back on again. This time Tommy brought the cinch up and pulled it just barely snug. Shadow fidgeted some more, but Tommy ignored it and, when the horse settled down, the saddle came off and the horse got a couple of pellets, his reward for good behavior.

The next day after he got home from school as usual, Tommy again saddled Shadow. When assured that the horse was accepting the saddle calmly, Tommy removed the hobbles, after first untying the halter shank. "We don't want a struggle here, if you get excited," he hold the horse. *Let him run, or buck, if he has to*, Tommy thought.

The stallion did not spook, however. Encouraged, Tommy tied the long rope to Shadow's halter, led him to the center of the pen, and then had the horse circle him a few times. Shadow watched those flapping stirrups, but otherwise did not get excited.

"Hey, that's good. Real good," Tommy said. He had stopped the horse and was petting him. "That's good enough for today," he said, and led Shadow back to the fence post and retied him, unsaddled, gave the horse a couple of pellets, and turned him loose. Tommy always wanted to do one new thing whenever he worked the horse, and when that one thing was accomplished, however little it might be, that ended the work for that day.

The ground work continued to go well. Tommy taught the horse to walk, then trot, then canter, in circles at the end of the rope, in response to voice commands. "That's so you'll know what I'm talking about, when I start riding you," Tommy explained to Shadow.

Things went so well that Tommy decided it was time to get on the horse. He wished his dad was there, just in case, but Al was still away, fighting a fire somewhere, and Tommy did not want to interrupt his training program.

And so the next day, while he was grooming the horse, he said, "Well, Shadow, you've graduated from elementary school. Now it's time to begin high school." Always talking to the horse, Tommy never let the stallion forget that something was going on.

It had been a while since Tommy had used the hobbles, but now he buckled them on again, after saddling the horse and circling him a few times on the long rope. Tommy untied the halter shank, took an extra turn around the post, and, still talking to Shadow, he took hold of a stirrup and tugged on it a bit. Then he put a foot in the stirrup.

A slightly turned head and a cocked ear showed that Shadow was watching, a bit skeptically. With his left hand, still holding the end of the halter shank, Tommy stroked Shadow's neck. His right hand was on the saddle horn. He gave a bit of a pull on the saddle horn, and then took his foot out of the stirrup.

He repeated that process once, and then the next time he slowly lifted himself off the ground. Shadow fidgeted, but Tommy stayed in the stirrup for about a minute before stepping down.

"Well, now," he said, "you're doing pretty good. Are you going to let me sit in the saddle this time?" Shadow seemed unconcerned.

Then, still holding the end of the halter rope in his left hand, so he could release the horse if he got in a panic, Tommy again stood up in the stirrup for a moment, and then, very carefully, he swung his leg over and was sitting in the saddle. Shadow shuffled his feet nervously, but Tommy kept talking, and stroking the stallion's neck, and the big horse calmed down.

Tommy dismounted, very slowly, and stood quietly for a minute, then he did it all one more time.

"That's enough for today, Shadow," Tommy said. "You're really doing great. We'll make a saddle horse out of you yet." He unsaddled, removed the hobbles, gave Shadow his reward, and turned him loose to roll. *That ground work really pays off*, Tommy thought.

The next day, after climbing on and off the horse a couple of times, Tommy removed the hobbles. He had put a hackamore on Shadow this time, and although he was standing by the familiar fence post, Shadow was not tied. Tommy got back in the saddle and then, very carefully, he pulled Shadow's head around and turned him away from the fence. Again, he got down and petted the horse. Now Shadow faced away from the fence, toward the center of the pen. *If he's ever going to run, he'll do it now*, Tommy thought. Hoping for the best, he got back in the saddle, and asked Shadow to walk, using the voice command. Shadow shuffled a bit nervously for a minute or so, and then he stepped out. Tommy let him walk a few steps, then turned back to the fence and walked the horse to the old familiar tying post. "Whoa, boy," Tommy said, and when Shadow stopped, he stepped off.

"Good boy, good boy," Tommy said, over and over, while he stroked Shadow's neck. It had been a good day. A little bit scary, but real good.

* * * * * * * * *

Some days Tommy didn't use the saddle. Using an overturned bucket to make it easier, he would lay on Shadow's bare back, then get astride. When the horse accepted that, Tommy began sliding off, and then getting back on, from the opposite, or off, side. He continued to think of something new and different, so that eventually the horse would be used to almost anything a rider might do. With the saddle, he mounted and dismounted from both sides, too. Tommy knew that sometimes, in rough country, or in a tight spot, he might have to get off the right side of the horse, and get back on from that same side. Anyway, he knew that his ancestors got on from the right side. His dad told him that in the old days if you saw a man get on his horse a mile away, you could tell whether it was a white man or an Indian because the white man always got on from the left side and the Indian from the right.

Tommy spent a lot of time "just fooling around," as he called it. He smiled when he thought about it, but he did not consider it a waste of time.

The stallion proved to be quite easy to train, it seemed, but Tommy knew it was only because he had patience, and took a whole lot more time with the horse than most trainers would want to do. Tommy knew, though, that in spite of his apparent success so far, the wild stallion was never far from flight. *One wrong move, one mistake*, Tommy told himself, *could be disastrous*. The stallion might panic, and then Tommy might forever have lost the horse's trust. Every move that Tommy made had that threat hanging over it.

Because of that threat, which caused Tommy to watch the big horse very closely, Tommy learned to read the horse's body language. *I think I'm learning as much as Shadow is*, Tommy reflected. *Maybe even more*.

It was only a matter of a few days more until Tommy could trot and canter the stallion, and then he could give the strong horse more exercise. He always tried to vary his program, by doing different things, and the stallion was responding nicely. "But this arena work is going to get tiresome for both of us," Tommy commented, as he put Shadow through some figure eights. "We need to get out of this pen once in a while. I wish Dad was here."

Chapter 13

MEXICO BILL

"Let the horse do all the fightin'."

Busy trying to persuade an old dude horse to leave the yard without the company of other horses, Tommy hadn't seen the rider approaching. He looked up and saw a tall, slender man, bronzed and mustached, sitting on a white horse. He smiled at Tommy.

"He's herd-bound. Won't go by himself," Tommy said.

"Point him where you want him to go," the stranger said, "then just sit on him. He'll stand there just so long, might try to turn back a time or two, but then he'll go of his own accord. It works every time."

Seeing Tommy's quizzical look, he added, "Call me Bill."

Mexico Bill! Tommy had heard about the Mexican who had come to Colorado's Western slope earlier that spring, and had soon made a name for himself wherever a rancher needed a top hand to help with his horses. He had heard, also, that Bill never said much about himself. His nickname came from more than just his bronzed complexion. Bill's attire, his equipment, and his working skills all spelled "vaquero," or, in Colorado, "buckaroo."

"Okay," Tommy said, "I'll try that later. Why don't you get down and get acquainted?" Tommy himself dismounted and tied his horse to the hitch-rail, and Bill did the same. Then Tommy held out his hand and said, "I'm Tommy Lewis."

"I'm pleased to meet you," Bill said. "Can you show me that wild horse I've been hearing about?"

"Sure. He's right here," Tommy said. They walked to the corral, and when Tommy called, the big bay stallion came trotting to him.

"Are you spoiling that horse?" Bill asked, and Tommy noticed the twinkle in Bill's eyes.

"I suppose I am. I feel kind of bad that he can't run wild anymore."

"I heard you have a way with horses," Bill said. "This is a beautiful animal. I can see why you wanted to protect him. Are you riding him yet?"

"Yes," Tommy said, "but so far, just in the pen." He entered the corral, grabbed a handful of mane, and spoke to the horse. Shadow turned and began to trot. Tommy jogged a couple of steps and then vaulted to the horse's back. Without saddle, bridle, or a halter, using only his voice, legs, and hands, Tommy cantered the horse once around the pen and came to a stop near Bill.

Bill whistled, and said, "You certainly do have a way with horses."

* * * * * * * * * *

"Come to the house and meet my parents," Tommy said. His father was home at the time.

"Mexico Bill," Al said, after Tommy had introduced him. "I'm gone a lot of the time, but I've heard about you. You don't object to the 'Mexico' part?"

"No, it suits me just fine," Bill smiled.

"You've seen the stallion?"

"Yes, and I've never seen a better one," Bill replied. "Tommy has done a fine job of handling that horse. What's it been, two months since you got him here?"

"That's about it," Al said. Then he looked at Bill. "Would you want to spend some time with us, and maybe give Tommy some help?"

"Well, yes, I can do that," Bill said. "I don't have any other work right now. I can bring my camper and stay for a while."

Tommy was overjoyed. He was certain he could find no better teacher. He had heard that the Mexican appeared equally at home in a stock saddle, working a reining or cutting horse, or astride a flat saddle, putting a gaited horse through its paces.

Bill moved his camper the next day. The trailer he pulled behind the camper held the blind white mare he called Snowball.

57

* * * * * * * * * *

For the rest of that fall, Tommy could hardly wait to get home from school each day, to ride with Bill. Snowball was good company for Shadow, and in a matter of days Tommy and Bill were out of the pen, riding the pastures and trails.

Tommy was amazed at what Snowball could do even though she was blind. When they came to a particularly bad place, with a lot of big rocks or holes, Bill would get off and walk ahead to pick out the best path, and Snowball followed with her nose in his back.

Discussing his approach to Shadow's training, Tommy said, "He learns fast. It seems almost like all he wants to know is what I want him to do. Having lived wild, he has a mind of his own, and I thought it would be wrong to try to force him to do anything."

"You're doing it exactly right," Bill said. "And that same method applies to all horses, not just to this particular one."

"I'm glad to hear you say that," Tommy said. "I probably went slower than I needed to, but I think that it would be pretty easy to upset Shadow, and if I did, then I would really have a problem."

"Yes, you would. And if that horse gets on the fight, no man can handle him. He'll do most anything for you, but I think if anybody else tried to ride him, the horse would go berserk. His confidence in you is not likely to carry over to other people."

* * * * * * * * * *

Bill helped Tommy work with the horses, but practiced with his ropes in his spare time. He had been asked to perform as a trick roper at the National Western Stock Show in Denver in January, and he had an idea.

"Why don't you come with me?" he asked Tommy. "You can put on a demonstration of Indian riding skills with Shadow. You know, just ride around bareback, without a bridle, and all that."

Tommy turned to stare at him, eyes wide. "Take Shadow to Denver? He's never been anywhere but in the mountains and here at the ranch. Wouldn't he be scared to death of all those people? And that big stadium?"

"Well," Bill replied, in his deliberate way, "I see more to the horse than that. He's wary, but not timid. He's smart and will adapt. He really is an exceptional horse. Given a chance, Shadow can make a name for himself. Shouldn't you let people see him?"

"Boy, I don't know about that!" Tommy said.

"Let's just leave it for a while. Think about it," Bill suggested.

Tommy could hardly say "no" to that, and, after a whole lot of discussion, his parents gave their consent. They had a lot of confidence in Mexico Bill.

* * * * * * * * * *

"We'll have to get Doc Morehouse out here," Al said. "Shadow will have to have some shots and he'll need a health certificate if he's going to the National Western."

The Glenwood Springs veterinarian came to the ranch a few days later. The stallion was leery of the stranger at first, but Doc was a horseman, and with Tommy at Shadow's head, petting and talking to him, he calmed down enough so Doc could give him the necessary shots and declare him fit.

Then Tommy said, "Doc, there's something I've been thinking about."

As Tommy explained, the veterinarian listened, smiled, and said, "Well, sure. Why not? It's a novel idea, but a pretty good one, at that."

It only took a few minutes more to do what Tommy had asked, and then Doc Morehouse stepped back, grinned, and said, "You've got interesting ideas, kid. Stick with them."

Chapter 14

AT THE NATIONAL WESTERN

Every event in the National Western rodeo was a thrill for Tommy. Having lived it all his fourteen years, he felt the adrenalin rush of every bronc rider as he mounted, the jolt of every jump the horse made, the pain of the rider who landed on his shoulders. He knew the thrill of every roper as his rope settled around the neck of a calf. But beyond that was his own anticipation, mixed with a hint of fear, as he waited impatiently for the break between the competitive events. His heart jumped as the announcer called out, "Ladies and gentlemen, here's Mexico Bill, expert horseman and rope artist, to entertain us. If you've never seen Bill, you have a thrill awaiting you!"

The arena lights dimmed and a spotlight followed Bill as he rode into the arena on Snowball. Spinning a gigantic loop around his horse, he cantered slowly around the arena, then went to the center and stopped. Still spinning his loop, Bill stood up on his saddle. He whirled the loop high above his head, let it fall until it brushed the ground, then lifted it again. He spoke to the mare, and she began walking, going first one way, then another, while Bill kept the big loop spinning.

Tommy wondered if those in the crowd who had never tried it realized what great skill and what a strong arm it required to accomplish that. And he knew that few, if any, realized that Snowball was blind. Perhaps they wondered why she wore goggles, not knowing they were to protect her eyes from the rope she couldn't see, as she followed Bill's every command.

Bill stopped the mare, dropped his rope, and dismounted. Tommy walked out, mounted Snowball, and moved away. Even though he had seen Bill practice many times he was entranced as Bill performed his rope spinning routine, more spectacular than most such acts because Bill used a sixty-foot Mexican maguey, or grass, rope that was much stiffer than the regular spinning ropes. Tommy had tried it and knew how difficult those throws were. In Bill's hands, that old grass rope seemed like it was alive, and had a mind of its own. Tommy was glad that although Bill dressed well, he shunned fancy clothes and silver mounted equipment. He let his performance speak for itself.

At a hand signal from Bill, Tommy galloped Snowball in a large circle. Bill's first catch was something seldom seen in any arena. He had a regular old butterfly going, and then with a vigorous sweep of his arm, he brought the loop around from behind his back and sent it flying almost halfway across the arena to settle neatly around Snowball's neck as she galloped past. The surprising, unusual throw, so beautifully done, brought the spectators to their feet.

Bill made a few more catches on the running horse, first the front legs, then the back legs, and then he motioned to the announcer.

"Wasn't that great?" the man with the microphone shouted. "And that's not all. Bill has a special treat for us. Have you heard about the young Indian lad who went into the mountains, in the White River National Forest, just last summer, and caught a wild stallion? He's here today, and he brought that wild horse he calls The Shadow Horse! Remember, this is his first public appearance, first time off the ranch, really, so I'm going to ask you to remain absolutely quiet until the performance is finished. Please do not applaud until I give you the okay. Are we ready?"

The arena lights dimmed, and the crowd quieted. Dressed in buckskins, Tommy walked to the center of the arena, sat down, and began playing his flute. The arena door opened, and the big mahogany bay stallion with luxuriously flowing black mane and tail stepped into the arena, unled and unfettered. He stood for a moment, looking regal, and then he walked slowly to the flute player. Tommy rose to his feet, pocketed the flute, placed a hand on the stallion's neck and together they began walking. Then the big horse broke into a trot, and so quickly that it surprised everyone, Tommy vaulted to the horse's sleek back.

Immediately the big horse broke into a gallop. With no saddle or bridle, not even a strap on the horse, Tommy slowed him to a canter. Then he turned in small circles, did a figure eight and reversed the direction of his circle. The perfectly balanced horse changed leads flawlessly. He executed every turn so precisely, so effortlessly and yet with great energy, that it all seemed more like play than something learned and rehearsed.

Again, responding only to Tommy's movements, unseen by others, Shadow broke into a fast gallop, then turned to run down the center of the arena. Just past the middle, the big horse slid to a graceful stop and Tommy leaped off. He walked to the arena gate, with Shadow closely following. Tommy's dad handed him a halter, and when that was buckled on and the horse led through the gate, Mexico Bill turned to the announcer and raised his hat.

At that signal, the man in the booth shouted, "All right! Let's hear it for Tommy Lewis and The Shadow Horse!"

Few in the stadium heard the last part of that sentence. As soon as they heard the "all right," the spectators began cheering, showing their appreciation for the beautifully done, unusual performance.

Tommy made sure Shadow was safely in a stall by himself before he joined his family to enjoy the rest of the rodeo. When it was over the Lewises went to a motel for the night, but Tommy bunked in the camper with Bill. He wanted to stay close to Shadow.

Chapter 15

LOST, STRAYED, OR STOLEN

"Bill! Bill!" Tommy sounded frantic.

Bill came charging out of the camper, hurriedly stuffing in his shirttail and buckling his belt. "What's wrong?" he asked.

"Shadow's gone!"

"Gone? What do you mean, he's gone?"

"He's just gone! I found his stall door wide open!"

Bill examined the door carefully, and said, "Somebody opened this door. The latch is horse-proof, and nothing's broken. Somebody has let him out, or taken him out. Let's take a quick look around. If we don't find him, we'll report it to the livestock superintendent."

They didn't find the stallion, and nobody they talked to remembered seeing a loose horse, or even hearing anything unusual during the night.

"I don't understand it," the superintendent said. "We have men patrolling the area. I'll look into it, and in the meantime I'll notify the sheriff and the brand inspector. What brand is he wearing?"

"He's not branded," Tommy said, and the superintendent sighed.

Tommy's parents went home to the ranch, knowing there was nothing they could do. But Bill and Tommy stayed in Denver, hoping somehow somebody might find a stray horse, or that the sheriff would learn something. But after two days with no news, Bill and Tommy had to give in and return home.

Driving down the interstate, Bill berated himself. "It's my fault," he said. "It was my crazy idea. I guess I had better learn to mind my own business." Tommy sat dejectedly. He had nothing to offer, and was afraid he might break down and cry if he even talked about it.

On Monday, he had to force himself to go to school. All week he avoided the other students. He was upset and angry with himself. *I went to Denver to show off*, he thought. And there were a dozen ranchers who had invested time and money in a corral. *What are they thinking now?* Tommy wondered.

* * * * * * * * * *

"Here comes our first unhappy visitor," Bill said with a wry smile, as Joe Morgan drove into the yard.

Morgan leaned on the gate and asked, "Is there any news of the stallion?"

"Not a thing. I wish I had never gone to that rodeo," Tommy said.

"I suppose you do," Morgan replied. "But look, maybe we'll find the horse. People will be on the lookout for him."

"Maybe," was all Tommy could come up with. He did not seem hopeful.

"Don't blame yourself," Morgan said. "Who would think a horse would be stolen out of a barn at the National?"

"Well, if I ever see that horse again, I'll know him," Tommy declared. "And I'll keep looking until I find him!" Seeing the determination in Tommy's eyes, Morgan knew that, if at all possible, Tommy would, some day, somehow, find the horse.

It was two days later when the telephone rang, and Al Lewis picked it up. It was Joe Morgan.

"Al," he said, "I've got some interesting news. There's talk about a big wild, dark bay horse that's making a name for himself as a bucker. They are going to feature him later this month at the Fort Worth stock show and rodeo. I think I'll go down there and take a look at that horse. I'll take Tommy if you think I should. How about it?"

"Well, I think if anybody ever put spurs to Shadow, he'd throw a fit, and it would be a good one. But I don't know," Al said. "There are a lot of bay horses."

"Yeah, I know," Morgan said. "But I want to go down there and take a look. Think about it, and I'll call you back."

* * * * * * * * * *

"Mind if I go with you to Fort Worth?" Bill asked, when Morgan arrived to discuss the trip.

"That is a great idea. We'll all go in my car," Morgan said.

"Well, I should drive down and take my trailer," Bill replied. "And I'll take Snowball. If that is Shadow, he'll be pretty wild and hard to handle. He'll load and ride a lot better with Snowball in the trailer."

"Yeah, you're right about that," Morgan agreed. Then he said, "In that case, I'll fly down. See you there, at the barns, on Saturday."

Chapter 16

THE MYSTERY HORSE

At the barns in Fort Worth, Tommy and Bill found that Morgan had reserved a stall for Snowball. Even though it was winter and quite cold in that part of Texas, they chose to sleep in the camper. Goose-down sleeping bags would keep them warm.

They had decided that they would not tell anyone why they were at the stock show. There was no use searching through the barns and pens. If the "owner" knew they were there, he might do something drastic.

* * * * * * * * *

Waiting for the mystery horse seemed like an eternity to Tommy, Bill, and Joe Morgan, sitting high in the grandstand. But at last the announcement came.

70

"Now, folks," the announcer said, "keep your eyes on Chute Number Six. The horse you have been waiting to see is being saddled, and you can see he's really putting up a fight!"

The chute gate swung open, and, bellowing and fighting as though he had a wildcat on his back, the big horse leaped into the arena. He made two lightning-fast, twisting jumps, so high and so vicious the rider didn't have a chance. When the cowboy hit the ground, arena attendants rushed out to drag him to safety, while both mounted pickup men put ropes on the lunging horse.

"What did I tell you?" the announcer shouted. "Isn't he something? We have decided to offer one thousand dollars to the first person that stays on him to the whistle!"

A shrill voice rang out, "I'll ride him!"

Chapter 17

TOMMY TAKES A CHANCE

"Tommy. Tommy. Take it easy." Bill held onto Tommy's arm and tried to calm him.

"I've found Shadow, and I'm going down there to get him!" Tommy declared. Yanking his arm free, he stood up and began making his way down through the crowd.

Everyone looked up to see who had spoken, and were surprised to see an Indian boy, his long hair hanging in two braids down the front of a buckskin shirt. Was it some kind of an act, they wondered? Tommy appeared to be very serious as he went down an aisle to the arena.

With a steady, confident stride, Tommy approached the announcer's booth. He looked up and said again, "I'll ride him."

"Are you kidding me?" the announcer asked. He shook his head, and said, "I don't think we can let some kid your age get on that horse. He's an outlaw. What makes you think you can ride him?"

"I can ride him!"

A big voice boomed from high in the stands, "Let the boy ride the horse!"

Standing in the top row of seats, Joe Morgan was an imposing sight. At six feet, three inches in his bare feet, and all of two hundred and forty pounds, he appeared positively gigantic in his boots and big hat.

The puzzled crowd remained silent. By then, the show manager had arrived at the booth. He took the microphone and said, "Folks, we don't know this boy. Is there somebody here who can take the responsibility for him?"

Coming down through the crowd, Morgan called out, "I will!"

"There's just one thing," Tommy said. "I'll do it my way. I want the horse stripped and the arena cleared. Don't put him in the bucking chute. And the crowd has to be quiet."

The baffled announcer looked at Tommy, but at a nod from the show manager he said, "Okay, we'll do it. Strip the horse, boys!" Arena attendants removed the association saddle, bucking strap, and halter from the big horse, who was still fighting to get away from them, and hastily exited the arena.

Wild-eyed, the stallion stood for a moment, every muscle taut. Then he whirled and tore around the arena, looking for a way out. Finding none, he charged the gate, crashed into it, and fell back, snorting and pawing the ground.

Mexico Bill had followed Joe Morgan out of the grandstand, and he said to Tommy, "Don't try to walk up to him. The horse is crazy with fear."

"I'm going to try to get him to come to me," Tommy replied.

"Okay," Bill said. "That might work. But be careful."

Then, without even looking at the wild horse, Tommy walked slowly to the center of the arena, sat down, and began softly playing the flute he had thought to bring with him. Somebody in the grandstand said, quietly but audibly, "It's one of those old, handmade Indian flutes."

Hearing the familiar sound of the flute, the stallion stood motionless, looking intently at Tommy. Then, slow step by slow step, he walked toward Tommy. Was he remembering?

The big horse stopped half a step away from the seated boy. Then he cautiously lowered his head, stretched out his neck, sniffed Tommy's buckskin shirt, and nickered.

"Hello, Shadow," Tommy said quietly. He turned, very slowly, and blew gently toward Shadow's nostrils. Then, as casually as he could manage, he stood up, pocketed the flute, and began walking away from the horse. The spellbound crowd watched breathlessly as the stallion followed the boy.

Tommy walked faster and, tossing his head, Shadow trotted up beside him. Tommy put one hand on the big horse's neck and jogged along for a few steps. Then so quickly and unexpectedly that it took everyone by surprise, Tommy vaulted to Shadow's back.

An involuntary gasp rose from the grandstand. Less than an hour ago, this same horse was a furious, savage brute, and now this youngster was on his back, without saddle or bridle. Not even a halter.

"Let's go, Shadow," he said, and the big horse broke into a gallop. He sped once around the arena and then, responding to Tommy's subtle command, he slowed to an easy canter. Then the previously unridable horse cantered gracefully in small circles, first one way, then the other, doing perfect figure eights and changing leads precisely and effortlessly with each change of direction. To all appearances, the boy and the horse were thoroughly enjoying themselves. Just playing, actually. It didn't look at all like some taught and laboriously practiced routine performed under a tight rein. It was almost a dance!

Then, abruptly, Shadow stopped, whirled, and dashed to the center of the arena, where he slid to a stop and reared. Standing almost straight up, he pawed the air like a boxer. Tommy's grip on the horse's mane kept him astride. When Shadow dropped to all fours Tommy slid off. He turned his back on the big horse and calmly walked to the exit gate, with the big stallion following closely.

Bill handed Tommy a halter, he buckled it on Shadow's head, Morgan opened the gate, and they all went out. Tommy reappeared a moment later. Amid wild applause, he strode to the announcer's booth. Real or an act, it had been a beautiful performance, and the crowd was pleased.

The show manager asked, "Are you putting us on? How did you do that?"

"It wasn't an act, or a trick," Tommy said. Then he explained. "The horse was stolen from me at Denver at the National Western show. He was running wild right up until Labor Day, when I caught him. He's real smart, learns fast. And he is naturally gentle. But he won't stand for any abuse. That's why he got so wild. I've been looking for the horse, and when I found him here, I took a chance and trusted to luck that he would remember me. That's all."

The show manager stared at Tommy and said, "That's quite a story, if it's true. Can you prove it?"

"I can prove it," Tommy replied, and said, "bring your show veterinarian out to the barn."

"Well, folks," the announcer said, "this is an amazing story. If we find that it's all true, Tommy will take that horse, and a check for a thousand dollars, home with him."

Chapter 18

ANOTHER INDIAN TRICK

At the barn, Mexico Bill and Joe Morgan stood back and let Tommy do his own talking. He seemed pretty sure of himself.

The Wyoming livestock contractor who furnished the rough stock for the rodeo said, "I don't know what's going on here, but I paid good money for that horse, and I have a bill of sale to prove it."

"Yes, but you bought a stolen horse," Tommy replied.

"The horse isn't even branded. The man I bought him from said he had just brought the horse in off the range. He told me the horse had been hiding out with a wild bunch, and had been hard to catch."

"He lied," Tommy said, and continued. "He took the horse out of a stall at the National, up at Denver. He probably thought he had a fine, well-trained horse, and then found out he couldn't handle the stallion. Do you think anybody could do what I just did with an unbroken horse?"

"No, of course not," the stock contractor said. "I'm puzzled. Some things don't add up here. I have a bill of sale, but if that horse does belong to you, then I want you to have him. Do you have papers, or anything else, to prove ownership?"

"I don't have a bill of sale," Tommy said. Then he explained that he had caught the horse in the mountains, and he did have a health certificate issued by Dr. Morehouse, from Glenwood Springs. "But, yes," he said, "I do have something else." Joe Morgan and Mexico Bill looked at each other and shrugged. They had no idea what Tommy was talking about.

Tommy turned to the veterinarian. "Doc," he said, "feel right here, on the neck."

The doctor felt where Tommy indicated. "I can feel something there, all right, just under the skin."

"That's a dime," Tommy said. "Dr. Morehouse put it there for me the same day he gave Shadow his shots and his health certificate. He'll testify to that, I'm sure. It's one of the last real silver dimes, and it's dated 1968. We can take it out if we need to." He couldn't help grinning at the look of amazement on the men's faces.

"Shall we call Dr. Morehouse?" he asked.

"Not necessary," the stock contractor said. "I'm convinced. It all adds up, finally. And don't worry Tommy. I know where to find that dealer, and I'll get my money back. You can bet on that! He's your horse, there's no doubt about it."

"Thanks," Tommy said, and they shook hands all around.

Then the show manager spoke up, and asked, "Could we get you to repeat that performance for tonight's show?"

"Well, this has been a real piece of luck for me," Tommy said. "I think we owe you something. What do you say, Bill? Do you have your ropes?"

"You know I never leave home without them," Bill said, and Tommy was pleased to see that the twinkle was back in the Mexican's eyes.

* * * * * * * * * *

When they found a stall for the stallion, Tommy declared, "I'm going to sleep with Shadow tonight."

"I thought you would," Bill said.

Joe Morgan spoke up. "Well," he said, "I have to say it again. This kid's still fulla surprises, ain't he? Bill, did you know about that dime?"

"No, I didn't," Bill replied. "And, yeah, he's fulla surprises. Tommy," he asked, "where did you get that idea?"

Tommy laughed. "Why," he said, "you guys should know by now. That's just another one of those old 'Indian' tricks."

II
SHADOW'S RUN

Published 2002 by Carl Mapps

Copyright 2002

Illustrations by Lloyd Mann

Carl Mapps

SHOT!

Riders who had chased him said that when the wild stallion went into timber, he disappeared, and it was no use trying to find him. They called him the shadow horse.

They said, too, that the Southern Ute Indian boy who caught the mustang in the mountains of Colorado's Western Slope is a natural-born horseman. Part horse, in cowboy lingo. Tommy Lewis scoffs at that notion. He says he just likes horses, that's all.

A year after that dramatic capture, Tommy and the shadow horse stood high on the the rim of a remote canyon in the White River National Forest. They might have been part of a Frederic Remington western painting. Intermittent stirring of the mahogany bay's luxurious black mane and tail, and sporadically trembling aspen leaves put life in the picture.

Tommy leaned forward, his two long braids swinging. He looked into the canyon and could hardly believe his eyes.

It wasn't spectacular scenery that amazed him. It was a herd of oddly-mixed cattle scattered on the canyon floor.

"Well, I wonder what those cows and calves are doing way out here?" Tommy mused, aloud. Shadow flicked an ear back, waiting.

Ranchers pastured cattle on forest service land, but there were no ranches anywhere near this remote area, that Tommy knew of. Could they be the cattle that had vanished from ranches on the other side of the mountain last summer?

Tommy recalled his father's words. "Probably trucked out," Al Lewis suggested. "That's the way they do it these days. It's so dry, tire tracks would hardly show." But had they, instead, been driven over the mountain?

"Let's see if we can find a way to get down there, Shadow," Tommy said. "I want to take a look at the brands on those cows."

He turned back and was shocked to find himself looking down the barrel of a rifle in the hands of a rough looking man standing in his path.

"Goin' somewhere, Sonny?" The scowling, trail-worn man spit tobacco juice at Shadow's feet.

"Ah…" Tommy stammered. His eyes shifted back to the black hole of the rifle's muzzle. He swallowed hard, trying to quell his surprise and fear, and managed to say, "I'm just on a little ride before school starts."

"An' doin' a little snoopin' while yer at it."

This is bad. Really bad, Tommy thought. *Those are the stolen cattle, and this guy is a rustler.* Trying to be casual, Tommy replied, "Snooping? I'm not snooping."

"Mebby not," the surly man retorted. "But I think we'll go down and see what the boss has to say. I doubt if he'll buy that story." He spat again, and added, with a smirk. "An he don't much like Indians, neither." Tommy wished he had tucked his braids under his hat, but it was too late for that.

Sensing Tommy's fear, Shadow tensed, nostrils flaring and eyes rolling. Equine instinct told him to turn and run from this belligerent, sour-smelling man. But behind him was a sheer drop off the canyon's rim. Trapped, the stallion crouched, nerves jumping, muscles taut.

When the menacing man motioned with his gun, the once-wild mustang heard again, from the summer before, the deafening explosion, and felt again the searing pain of a glancing bullet. With no way out, he lunged, lightning-quick. The man blocking his way jerked the trigger as he went down under the stallion's thrashing hooves.

When his horse leaped, Tommy lost both stirrups. He grabbed his saddle horn a split second before hearing the crack of the rifle and getting a jolting blow that nearly took him out of his saddle.

Shadow hurdled the fallen man and fled down the trail. Tommy dug his heels into Shadow's sides, letting his stirrups flap. His mind raced along with his horse, his only thought was *Get away! We have to get away!* "GO, SHADOW, GO!" he called.

Tommy knew that few horses could match the speed and endurance of the shadow horse. Safety was just a few short miles away. But something was wrong. Waves of pain shot through his body with every pounding stride. It seemed like a red-hot knife stabbed him, over and over again. Reluctantly, and with considerable difficulty, he slowed the frightened horse.

Barely able to restrain the frantic stallion, Tommy said, "Easy, boy. I don't know what's wrong, but I can't stand the pounding." His left side, just above the belt, felt warm and wet.

Blood! he thought. *I think I've been shot!*

He couldn't believe it. Nobody had ever pointed a gun at him, not even in play. Were the threatening man, Shadow's leap, the gunshot and the wild dash down the trail all just a nightmare? Blood and pain said it was not a dream.

He left the trail and found partial shelter behind a pile of boulders, remnants of a long-ago rock slide, and got down. Standing on shaking legs, he yanked open his shirt. His worst fears realized, his knees went weak at the sight of a ragged, bloody gash.

Tommy had been injured, lots of times. That didn't bother him. But now he knew fear. A man had tried to kill him. Other men, dangerous outlaws, would be searching for him, might at that very moment be coming down the trail, riding hard.

Was he to be hunted down, like a wounded animal? On the verge of panic, Tommy thought of his parents. They had trusted his judgment, and he'd let them down. So thinking, he recalled his father saying, "Bad things happen. You have to stay calm. Let your head get you out of trouble when your legs can't." Tommy smiled at the recollection. He wasn't done yet.

He dug his first aid kit out of a saddlebag. Then, using his torn shirttail for a rag, he wiped up most of the blood. Luckily, the bullet had not gone clear through him. *It looks like it glanced off my rib. The rib's broken; that's what's so painful. But I'm lucky.* He shuddered at the thought of a bullet going through his body.

He soaked a gauze pad with disinfectant and winced when he taped it over the wound. *That will stay on for about a minute,* he thought. *I need something to wrap around me.*

He usually carried a roller bandage in his saddlebags. He kept it in case his horse hurt a leg a long way from home, or for just anything, for that matter. Was it still there?

Tommy hunted through the saddlebags and, yes, there it was, right where it was supposed to be! He hadn't needed it all summer, and had all but forgotten about it.

He wrapped the bandage around his waist a couple of times, pinned it, and thought, *that will help a lot. Now maybe I can ride.* "Now Shadow," he said, "if you can stand still long enough for me to get back on, we'll go on down the trail."

He led the anxious, fretting horse to a rock he could stand on to make mounting easier, and got on. The effort made his head swim, and pain surged through his side. He waited a minute to let his head clear, then rode back to the trail.

He glanced up and down the trail, and listened for a moment, before riding out into the open. "Okay, Shadow," he said, "let's go. We have a head start, but we don't know how much. I hope I can stand to ride faster than a walk."

All he needed to do was give Shadow his head, and the eager horse went to his easy, ground-eating lope. He could go for miles at that pace. But then Tommy's wound began to bleed, and the pain, though diminished, was still there.

"I can't do it, Shadow," Tommy said, again slowing the horse. "We have to walk. We'll go faster when we have to, but only then."

Was he going to get a bullet in the back? He could almost feel it coming.

There was some comfort in knowing that the mustang, with his finely-tuned senses, would detect an approaching horseman long before he himself could. It wasn't much, but it was something.

2. THE SHADOW HORSE GOES HOME

Tommy listened for pounding hooves of fast-running horses. How long had it taken, after the gunshot, for somebody to find the trampled rustler? And how badly was that man hurt? Could he describe Tommy and his horse? The only thing Tommy knew for sure was that the rustlers would make every effort to find him.

Those guys will shoot me on sight, Tommy mused. *They'll stop at nothing to prevent me from spoiling their scheme, and here I am, my horse walking down the trail. I'm a dude on a sightseeing trip. Should I be riding hard? Could I stand the pain?*

Should he get off the trail, ride where he couldn't be seen? *No. That won't work. Too slow, and when it gets dark I won't be able to move at all. My best bet is to stay on the trail and make a run for it if I have to.*

The sun dropped behind the mountains and Tommy felt a lot safer. *Now, at least I won't be such an easy target,* he thought, *and that cool night air really feels good.*

But he was tired, and feeling a little bit sick. Tommy had heard stories about riders falling asleep while they rode. Could it come to that? He had a long ride ahead of him. He knotted his long reins so they would hang over Shadow's neck. *Just in case,* he told himself. When he had stopped to tend his wound, he'd thought to tie his mecate around Shadow's neck, run it through the noseband of the bridle, and stuff the rest of the rope under his belt. That way, if he fell off, for whatever reason, he had a chance to hang onto his horse.

Determined to keep going, Tommy clutched the saddle horn with both hands, and thought, *All I have to do is stay on. Shadow can follow the trail in the dark. He knows the way, and he'll go home. Horses always go home.*

And he was right; the shadow horse went home. Tommy didn't know it, but the mustang was in familiar territory. Left to find his own way, Shadow left the trail and went to a secluded little valley nearby. It was where he and his band of mares always spent the winter when they were still free. The shadow horse was home.

The hypnotic walking motion stopped, and Tommy thumped Shadow's sides with his bootheels. "Come on," he said. "Let's go. We can't stop."

Shadow didn't move, and Tommy thumped some more. Then Shadow dropped his head, and

Tommy realized he was drinking water. *So that's it*, he thought. *He found water, and he's thirsty. And I'm thirsty, too. I better get a drink. My canteen's empty.*

He slid out of his saddle and stood on shaking legs. He'd been riding too long. He knelt beside Shadow's forelegs, and suddenly realized that, with his broken rib, he could not lean down to drink from the spring.

It seemed to take all of his strength to pull himself to his feet. *Man*, he thought, *I'm weak*. He took his canteen from the saddlebag and was reminded of the need for water pills. *All I need now, to add to my troubles, is a dose of beaver fever*. The sickness, also called backpacker's flu, resulted from drinking water contaminated by a parasite carried by beavers. He found the little bottle of pills and dropped one into his canteen.

He knelt again, shoved the canteen under water to fill, then took a long drink. He let the canteen fill again, and got to his feet, this time with a little less effort. The water made him feel better, and his stiffened muscles were working better.

I think I'm ready to ride again, he thought. *That water made me feel a whole lot better. We'll be off the mountain by daylight.*

Wanting to let some air under the saddle blanket and reset his saddle, Tommy loosened the cinch. But when he tried to lift the saddle, he found he couldn't do it. The overlong ride, the loss of blood, and nothing to eat or drink since that morning, had taken more out of him than he'd realized.

Tommy snugged up the cinch, and said, "Sorry, Shadow. I can't do it. We're gonna have to tough it out." His irritation subsided as he stroked the stallion's sleek neck. "You're taking good care of me, Shadow," he said. "I was too dumb to know I needed that drink. Well, let's get going."

Tommy got his foot half way to the stirrup and changed his mind. No amount of determination could overcome the pain and weakness.

"We'll have to say here and rest, Shadow," he said. He could see, in the starlight, that the spring was at one end of a little meadow, surrounded by pine forest. What looked like a grove of scrub oak was only a few steps away.

He led Shadow to the grove and was pleased to see a lot of young oak underbrush within the grove.

"This looks pretty good, Shadow. I can hide in there, and there's plenty of grass here for you." He knelt again, and buckled hobbles on Shadow's front legs. Then he removed saddle and bridle and dragged his gear into the thicket.

He found space to unroll his bed, and thought, *Man, it's gonna feel good to lie down and rest.* But something bothered him. What? he wondered. Pondering over whether or not he ought to try to take his boots off, it came to him. *The hobbles! If somebody comes here looking for me and sees a hobbled horse, I'm a gonner.*

Tired almost beyond belief, Tommy forced himself to crawl out of the thicket and go to Shadow. A sickle moon had come up, and in the better light, Tommy saw the sweatmarks.

What next? he wondered, with a sinking heart. *Another dead giveaway. I have to clean him up.* Would this nightmare never end?

Tommy had no grooming equipment, not even a brush. *I'll use my shirt for a rub rag. It's a mess, anyway. But it's gonna be a job. I'm too tired to do this; I wish I could give him a bath.* Then he smiled. He would, in fact, give the horse a bath. It would be easier, and better.

He went back to his shelter, found his cookpot, and went to the spring. He laid his filthy shirt on the ground and ladled water onto it. That way, he wasn't contaminating the spring. Then, with the soaked shirt and a pot full of water he went to the horse.

Shadow flinched when the cold water first hit him, then he relaxed and seemed to enjoy his bath.

"Yeah, that ought to feel good," Tommy remarked. "You were a mess, all right." He made two more trips to the spring, and, with surprisingly little effort, cleaned Shadow's sweaty hide. "There you go, Shadow," he said. "All cleaned up. Now, I'll take the hobbles off." Shadow turned his head, and Tommy said, "Oh, yeah, you're looking for a treat. I don't know if I have any of those pellets left." He felt through his pockets, found one, and gave it to the stallion.

Tommy walked back to his shelter, and thought, *This is the first time I've turned him loose in the wide open spaces.* Would the call of the wild reclaim the once-wild mustang?

I can't worry about that now. I don't dare make mistakes. Those rustlers won't be easily fooled. I have

*to outwit them if I expect to get out of this particular
fix.*

He crawled into his shelter and spread his shirt,
now a lot cleaner, out to dry. Then he put on an old
sweatshirt, lay down on his bed, and covered himself
with a blanket. Nights were cool, at that altitude.

He sighed with relief as his aching body began
to relax. Had he forgotten anything? Would Shadow
still be there in the morning? Would the rustlers find
him? His eyes closed without his knowing it, even as
he asked himself those questions, and sleep did not
wait for answers.

Carl Mapps

3. TRAPPED

The warming sun woke him. Tommy lay still, listening.

Chirping birds, busily flitting about, seemed undisturbed. Reassured, Tommy yawned, stretched, and started to crawl out of the thicket. He stopped abruptly when he heard voices. He watched two men ride into the clearing. They had their rifles in their hands.

Tommy sucked in his breath. Rustlers! Hunting for him!

Suddenly one man exclaimed, "Look! There's a horse!" Tommy looked where the man pointed and saw Shadow just disappearing into the woods.

"Recon that's a wild horse?"

"Maybe," the second man replied. "Adam said the kid rode a barefoot horse. but that he took off on a dead run. It don't seem like he'd of been walking his horse, does it? And why would he come here and turn his horse loose? That don't make no sense."

"Yeah, I think we've been tracking the wrong horse. Let's get back on the trail. We have to catch that Indian kid."

Heart racing, Tommy watched the two men ride away.

He let his breath out slowly, and thought, *That was close. Too close! It's a good thing I gave Shadow a bath and took the hobbles off. Those guys know who to look for; he said "that Indian kid." And the man Shadow ran over is alive. They called him Adam. I'm safe here, for now, but I'm trapped. I don't dare go back to the trail; I'd hate to meet those armed men.*

He waited a few minutes, then crawled out and looked around. The riders were gone, and the shadow horse was still living up to his name.

Tommy filled his canteen and returned to his shelter. He sat quietly, munching trail mix and jerky. He changed his bandage, then got up and walked around. He was stiff and sore, but felt his strength returning. But having to hide, unable to do anything, was frustrating.

How long was he going to have to hide? And what was there about the week before Labor Day? This same time last summer, he had just caught the injured wild stallion and had a man with a broken leg in camp. A long way from home and needing help, he had gotten it Indian style; with a signal fire.

But that time, Steven Peterson was keeping an eye on the sky. When he saw the smoke, he knew Tommy wanted help. Now, however, he was on his own.

And yet, that was not exactly true. Fire danger was high. Lookouts manned observation towers. They would see smoke, and likely a small plane or a chopper would come to investigate.

Tommy was aware that he would be in trouble if he built a fire. The forest service took a dim view of deliberately set fires. Tommy ought to know; his dad worked for the forest service. Was fighting a fire in Idaho when Tommly had left on his little overnight ride. And if the rustlers came first? Tommy shuddered at the thought.

Here I sit, he brooded. *I've found the cattle, and I can't do a thing about it. By the time I get home and notify the sheriff, the rustlers will have moved the cattle, But what can I do*? He struggled with his thoughts until he was tired of it. How far down the trail had those two rustlers gone? If he built a fire, and the rustlers were far enough away, a chopper would get here first. If a chopper came.

It's a long shot, Tommy thought. *But if I sit here, knowing what I do, and those rustlers get away with the cattle because I'm afraid to take a chance, I'll never forgive myself. I'm gonna build a fire*!

4. SMOKE SIGNAL

Determined to do something, right or wrong, Tommy found an open spot. He scuffed away what little grass and debris there was with his booted feet. There was little danger of the fire spreading, unless he made the fire too big, or a strong wind came up. He could control the size of the fire, and could only hope the day remained calm.

Dead, dry branches littered the ground under trees. It was only a matter of minutes to gather enough small stuff to get the blaze started. Gathering wood off the ground was a little bit difficult, with a broken rib, but Tommy did not expect it to be easy. He bent his knees, kept his back upright, and reached for the wood.

When he had a good fire going, had added some larger dry wood to make the green wood burn, he began cutting green branches from pine trees. Again, it was not easy, and it made his side hurt, but with the folding camp saw he always brought with him on a camping trip, he got the job done. He would not have been able to do it with an axe; not with a broken rib.

Cutting those lower branches did very little damage, if any, to the trees. As the trees grew taller, those lower branches always fell off anyway.

When he had collected a good armful of the green wood, Tommy threw it all on the fire. Then he stood back to watch his smoke signal. The green wood began to burn, and a column of black smoke spiraled high in the still air.

That's perfect! Tommy mused. *It's a good day for a smoke signal. I'm gonna have company now.* Who would come first, the rustlers, or the forest service? Everything depended on that.

He let the fire die down to coals, then went back to his shelter. He wanted to see who his visitors were before they saw him.

But what could he do, if the rustlers came first? Drag his gear into the woods and try to hide? *There's no use doing that*, he thought. *They would find me*. He decided to go into the woods where he had seen Shadow disappear. Maybe he could find the horse and, if necessary, escape riding bareback. He shuddered at the thought. *More likely,* he mused, *I'll just try to get away in the woods. Even if those men come back here, and start looking for me, they'll run if they hear a chopper. It's my only hope.*

Tommy didn't know he had fallen asleep. He just wanted to lie down and rest for a few minutes before going deeper into the woods. He woke up with a start. Had he heard a helicopter? He listened, and heard only twittering birds and a chittering chipmunk. *It was just a dream, I guess*, he decided. *Wishful thinking.*

He crawled out of the thicket and looked around. There were no riders in sight, no helicopter, and no shadow horse. Then he heard it again; the unmistakable, rhythmic beat of rotor blades.

Excited, Tommy hurried to his shelter. He grabbed his shirt and went back to the clearing, waving his shirt around and around over his head as soon as he saw the chopper.

The big bird flew over the clearing down at the far end and kept on going. *They didn't see me! They're looking for smoke; I should have kept the fire going.* Tommy's spirit fell along with his arm as he dropped it to his side.

He watched, unbelieving, as the chopper flew out of sight. Then he trudged back to his shelter, dragging his shirt. He thought, *Well, that's that. I tried, but didn't go a good enough job of it. My only hope now is that if the rustlers see the chopper, they'll try to get away. But they will know who started the fire; they'll really be after me now. Maybe the shadow horse and I will have to hide out for a while longer.*

Wondering what else could happen, Tommy began crawling into his shelter, then he stopped. Was the chopper coming back? He got back on his feet, listening, then shouted, "Yes! It's coming back. There it is!" Again, he whirled his shirt. The aircraft changed course, came closer, and settled to the ground.

A man wearing the forest service uniform got out of the chopper. Tommy recognized George Thompson, a friend of his father.

Thompson looked surprised. "Tommy Lewis!" he exclaimed. "I didn't expect to find you here. Somebody reported seeing smoke out here somewhere. What's going on?"

"My fire," Tommy replied, "And, man, you don't know how glad I am to see you." Then he explained, as briefly as possible, why he had sent up the smoke.

Thompson frowned, and said, "Boy, you've had a time, all right. And you got shot? Are you okay?"

"It's just a flesh wound. And a sore rib. But I'm okay. I can ride home now, if the rustlers are no longer a threat. I didn't know how long I might have to hide, and how long it was going to take me to get home to notify the sheriff about the cattle. Figured we might lose the cattle."

"Yeah, I think you're right. The forest service doesn't much like to have people start fires, but in this case, I think you are entirely justified." He grinned, and went on, "I'll get my map, so we can get oriented here." He went to the helicopter and came back with his big topographical map.

Thompson spread the map on the ground, and said, "Here's where we are now," and pointed.

"Okay," Tommy replied. "and this is the canyon where I saw the cows." He pointed, and Thompson marked the canyon with a highlighter. "Good," he said. "I'll go call the sheriff."

He returned to the aircraft, and came back in a few minutes, smiling. "He said two big choppers would be here in real short order. Why don't you come back with us?"

"Well, I'm not worried about getting home now. And I'd have to come back up here to get my horse, anyway. Call my folks and tell them I'll start home tomorrow."

"All right, I'll do that. Your dad is still on a fire up in Idaho. But your mom will be glad to know. By the way, where's your horse, anyway? I don't see him."

"He's in the woods. We both had to hide. And hey, I'm sorry about the fire."

Chuckling, Thompson said, "You're beginning to get a reputation for sending up smoke signals."

"Yeah, I just got over being kidded about that, and now it will start all over again. Well, I really appreciate your coming up here. Glad it was you. Somebody else might not have been so understanding."

"No problem," Thompson replied. He shook hands, patted Tommy on the shoulder, and asked, "You're sure you're okay?"

"I'm fine. More than fine now. I feel wonderful."

"Good. Well, we'll check to make sure your fire is all cold, and be on our way. You take care now, Tommy."

A few minutes later, Tommy watched the little aircraft lift off and fly back to civilization. It was barely out of sight when two big police choppers appeared, thrashing their way toward the canyon. *Beautiful*, Tommy thought. *Ugly machines, but right now, they're beautiful.*

Carl Mapps

5. THE CONCERT IN THE CLEARING

I can ride home tomorrow! Tommy could hardly believe it. By tomorrow, the rustlers would have been captured, or would be running for their lives. They would no longer be gunning for "that Indian kid." Tommy went to his shelter, stretched out on his bed, and tried to take it all in. An awful lot had happened in the last twenty four hours.

It was no surprise that Shadow had not come out of the woods. Why would he? The same instincts that prompted him to run into the woods when riders appeared would tell him to hide from an intrusive helicopter, and strange men.

Would he ever come back? Tommy wondered. Had recent traumatic events driven the mustang back to the wilderness? *I really don't blame him, if he's decided he's had enough of civilization*, Tommy mused. *But I hate to think I've lost him. That horse is family, to me.*

If he were asked, Tommy would say that he wished the mustang stallion could always live wild, as nature intended. He had only gone out to try to catch the horse to save him from certain death at the hands of irate ranchers who had lost good mares to the wild and wiley stallion.

Tommy tried to tell himself that only time would tell if the shadow horse was going to come back to the clearing. But he knew he wouldn't rest until he found out, one way or another. *There's no use going out to try to find him in the woods*, Tommy concluded. *I'll see if I can call him out with my flute.*

He had played the flute to give himself a non-threatening identity with the horses when he worked his way into the wild band. And he had played it again, to calm the frenzied stallion, in the arena at the Fort Worth rodeo, just the past winter.

Shadow had been stolen and sold to a rodeo stock contractor, and was advertised as a mystery bucker at the Fort Worth rodeo. A thousand dollars had been offered to the first person to ride the wild horse to the whistle.

After he called the frightened and confused stallion to him with the flute, Tommy rode him, bareback, without a strap on the horse. He rode him for fifteen minutes, cantering in circles and figure eights, all done playfully but in perfect control. He rode the horse fast, around the arena, mane and tail flying, a beautiful sight that brought the spectators to their feet. When the running horse slid to a stop and reared, with no apparent signal, Tommy slid off and walked to the gate, with the big bay following. He went home with his horse, and the money. *Yeah*, Tommy thought, *the flute will bring him out of the woods if anything will*.

He went out just before dark, carrying the little wooden flute that his grandfather had made. He intended to play a bird call, something natural. He did not intend to go out shouting for all the world to hear. *I think those rustlers would like to get a shot at me*, he thought, with a rueful grin.

Tommy skirted the edge of the woods, playing the beautiful, haunting song of the mourning dove. He loved that above all other bird calls. Had practiced it while riding Shadow on the mountain. If he could hear it, Shadow would know it was Tommy.

He walked slowly, down, and back, playing the song in all of its several variations, but the horse did not come. He stood where he had seen Shadow run into the woods that morning, and played some more, still with no success. Was the plaintive song of the mourning dove to be his farewell to the shadow horse? Dejected, Tommy thought, *I'll try again in the morning*.

He plodded back toward his shelter, half-heartedly tootling a nonsensical tune on the flute, and failed to hear grass-muffled footsteps behind him. Then a hard shove at the middle of his back sent him sprawling face down. Pain shot through his side and took his breath away.

Caught, after all! He had been careless. Expecting a gunshot, or a blow to the head from a gunstock, Tommy looked back to see his attacker. Looming over him, looking at him, Shadow tossed his head.

Barely able to comprehend all that had happened, Tommy struggled to his feet. When his heart stopped pounding, and he could breathe again, he stroked Shadow's neck and said, "You came back." Then he choked. Tears of relief and joy filled his eyes, and Tommy was ashamed. He was ashamed because Indian boys a step away from manhood do not cry, and he was doubly ashamed for having doubted the loyalty of the shadow horse.

Before starting for home the next morning, Tommy sat his saddle and took a last look at the beautiful little valley. "We'll be back, Shadow," he said. He turned the mustang and rode toward the rising sun.

By the looks of the sun, it was about noon when Tommy saw a rider coming toward him on the trail. Still cautious, he rode off the trail into some brush. Soon Tommy recognized his good friend and neighbor, Steven Peterson. *Steve's growing fast. Gonna be big like his dad*, Tommy mused. Two years younger than Tommy, Steve already was taller. *I'll surprise him*, Tommy decided. But Shadow spoiled the plan when he nickered a greeting at Diamond Lil. Tommy rode out and said, "Hi, Steve. Looking for somebody?"

"Yeah. You," Steve said, grinning. "Your mom wanted me to come up here and see if I can get you home."

"Well, you found me," Tommy replied. "Did she say whether or not the sheriff caught the rustlers?"

"No, and I didn't wait around to find out. Do you look for trouble, or does trouble look for you?"

"I wish I knew."

Time and miles flew by as the two friends chatted. They got to the beaver pond late that afternoon, and Tommy asked, "Want to stay here tonight and go home tomorrow?"

"Suits me," Steve replied. "I don't much like the thought of going down that steep canyon trail in the dark. Don't even like to go down it in the daytime."

"I don't either," Tommy admitted. "And I haven't had a decent meal for several days. Let's camp. I have some fish line, and hooks. We'll catch a couple of rainbows and have a picnic."

Carl Mapps

6. INDIAN SUMMER

One Saturday in October, Tommy Lewis and Steve Peterson rode through the high mountain pastures. They were looking for strays, cattle that were missed in the fall gather. Unable to survive the winter on the mountain, they had to be found and brought down.

The boys knew the mountain pastures well. They had ridden there since they were old enough to ride. They liked hunting strays, and ranchers appreciated the help. Now the two boys were letting their horses graze the nutritious mature mountain meadow grass, and Steve asked, "How come they call it Indian Summer?"

"I don't know," Tommy replied. "It goes way back, I guess. But it's a nice time to be up here. Best time of the year, really. Especially this year. Reporters still come around on weekends, when I'm not in school. They're okay people, but it gets tiresome."

"Well, you're a celebrity!"

"Some celebrity!" Tommy laughed, and said. "I stumbled onto the stolen cattle by accident, got myself shot, and then ran and hid. I even broke the law when I built a fire. And to top it all off, the rustlers escaped. I guess the helicopters scared them away."

"Yeah, that was too bad. Dad says someone wants to buy Shadow. You won't sell him, will you?"

"No way!" Tommy exclaimed. "Anyway, who really owns him? The Bureau of Land Management gave us a bill of sale for the horse. But half a dozen ranchers built his corral and the shed. They donated all the material and did all the work. Shadow belongs to all of us. And he belongs here, in the valley. I'd hate to think of him living in a box stall on a horse farm back East. Maybe get turned out in a paddock once a day. It would be like being cooped up in school."

"Yeah, you're right about that."

"But hey," Tommy continued, "I have to admit that now I kind of like school. High School is more interesting than grade school. I like the classes. And there are a lot of things to do, like sports. I think you'll like it better when you get there next year."

"Yeah, maybe. It's too bad you had to sit out the cross country races this year."

"Yes, I missed that. But my broken rib is healed, and I'm running again. Just on my own. Well, we better start looking for strays. What say we split up and go around both sides of that big draw. We can meet at the rock slide, and come back down through the draw."

They found no cattle going up, but, as they expected, found several cows, each one with a calf, hiding in the draw when they rode through it on the way down. Those pairs they drove to a holding pen in one corner of the meadow. They had time to search for more strays before starting down with what they had found. They would take the cattle to the Peterson ranch, where they would be picked up by their respective owners.

At supper that evening, Tommy asked, "Dad, do you know Tommy John?"

"I know an Indian by that name. He lives at the Jemez Pueblo in New Mexico. Works for the forest service. I see him once in a while, usually on a fire. Why do you ask?"

"Our cross country coach told us about him. Said he's a long distance runner who likes the mountain runs, like the Pikes Peak Marathon. Every summer, if he has the time, he goes on what he calls a cleansing run. He wears just shorts and running shoes, and takes nothing with him. He stays out for several days, drinking from springs and eating what berries he finds. He says it's spiritually and physically cleansing."

"Well, that's interesting," Al Lewis replied. "I'm not surprised. Tom doesn't talk about that. But he's a serious guy. More traditional Native American than most of us."

"I like that idea," Tommy said. "It's kind of like a vision quest." Noticing his mother's quick, "Oh, no!" glance at her husband, Tommy laughed. "Don't worry, Mom," he said. I'm not going to do anything foolish."

Smiling, Betty Lewis said, "I'll stop worrying when you stop chasing after outlaws and going out to catch wild horses all by yourself." Tommy saw the worry behind the smile.

It was Tommy's habit to go out after supper to see the horses. He looked them over, talked to each horse, and gave it a pelleted grain treat. While he was with the other horses, the stallion stood apart, waiting his turn.

Tommy ran his hands over Shadow's neck and back. "You're beginning to grow your winter coat, Shadow," he said. The stallion turned his head and nuzzled Tommy. "And now you're looking for a treat. You're spoiled, all right." He fished the last two pellets out of his pocket. "There you go," he said. He gave Shadow a pat on the rump and left the corral.

On his way back to the house, Tommy couldn't get the notion of the cleansing run out of his head. *Only a couple of generations ago young Indians looking for spiritual guidance and an identity went on vision quests.* Then, recalling his father's comment on the subject. "Nowdays," Al Lewis had said, "they bum around Europe trying to 'find' themselves." Tommy laughed. He opened the screen door at the back of the house and stepped inside. It was time to think about tomorrow's algebra test. Algebra was one tough subject.

7. THE CLEANSING RUN

Tommy went out the door at daylight on the first Thursday in November. The annual teachers' conferences gave him the four-day weekend he needed for his cleansing run. Standing by the door, Al Lewis said only, "Watch the weather." Tommy smiled, nodded, and was gone.

He was just mildly surprised when his parents gave their okay. Betty Lewis had said, "I don't know why boys have to do so many things to worry their mothers."

"Fathers worry too," Al Lewis replied. He put an arm around Betty's shoulders and said, "I'll help you worry." Both smiled, but Tommy knew they would worry. He knew also that they had confidence in his judgment and abilities; his father had taught him well.

As Southern Utes, Al and Betty Lewis respected and valued many traditional Native American ways. "Times have changed, but people are the same," Al Lewis declared. "Boys like challenges. Testing themselves is part of growing up."

A cloudless sky promised a beautiful day. When he left the house, Tommy wore old running shoes, winter underwear, and a sweatsuit. In a small backpack he carried a light wind and rain resistant jacket, a small survival blanket, cotton gloves, and a bright orange stocking cap. Bowhunters were still out, and he didn't want to be mistaken for a deer.

He also had a compass, scout knife, matches in a waterproof container, packages of trail mix and jerky, and the customary water pills for purifying drinking water. There would be, he knew, the inevitable bar of soap. His mother always made sure of that. Tommy smiled, thinking of the many times the soap had proved to be valuable. Most notable was the summer before, when he had caught the wild stallion, and needed to clean up a ragged, dirt filled bullet wound on the horse's shoulder. Tommy had no medical supplies, but soap had done the job.

He would not have taken so much with him in July or August. Probably not in September. But the weather could change, rapidly and drastically, in November. The mountains were notoriously unforgiving of mistakes. One needed to respect the mountains.

Tommy felt good. His rib had healed, and he was in excellent condition.

But this was not a race. There was no need to see how far, or how fast, he could go. And he knew better than to wear himself out just getting up the mountain the first day. He took it easy, alternated walking and jogging. Even so, he soon shed his sweatshirt under the warming sun.

Tommy didn't mind sweating, but he didn't want to get to the beaver pond soaked with sweat. *Too many hikers have done that*, he reflected. *Then they sit down to rest, cool off too fast, and get disoriented. They sit there in a stupor and die of hypothermia, with a warm jacket, maybe a sleeping bag, in their backpack.*

He arrived at the beaver pond a little before noon, and rested. From there, it was only a couple of miles, and easy going, to the little valley where he planned to stay the first night.

When he got to the bluff overlooking the valley, Tommy stood for a while, remembering his wild ride on Old Bess. It had been a year ago, just before Labor Day, when he was trying to catch the wild stallion. He had worked his way into the broodmare band, and could pet most of the mares. Some had been on ranches, and were used to people, even broke to ride. Old Bess was one of those.

Tommy had been petting Old Bess when rancher Joe Morgan came, riding fast. The wild horses had fled danger many times, and when they saw the rider approaching they all took off.

Not wanting to be trampled, Tommy swung onto Old Bess's back when she turned to run. Head down and eyes shut against the dust, Tommy looked up and was horrified to see the horses running full speed over the edge of the bluff.

Old Bess, too, went over without slackening her pace. She plunged down the slope, keeping her feet until Joe Morgan's riderless horse crashed into her from behind. Bess tumbled, and Tommy went flying. He hit something solid and blacked out.

When he regained consciousness, Tommy was confronted with a strange sight. Joe Morgan lay up the slope, with a broken leg. Below Tommy, Morgan's horse lay, also with a broken leg. A little farther down, the stallion lay, also badly injured. Down on the valley floor, the mares and foals grazed peacefully, as if nothing had happened.

It was a day Tommy hoped never to have to do over. And yet, much good had come of it. He got his ropes on the wild stallion, got help with his smoke signal, and became a very good friend of Joe Morgan's. The road to those successes had been rocky, to put it mildly. Yes, it was a day to remember. But now, laughing, sliding and leaping, Tommy went down the slope in his own little cloud of dust.

At the bottom, Tommy turned to his right and dropped his pack under some young spruces. He drank from his canteen, then went to the little stream to refill it. *Beaver country,* he remembered, *I'll use a water pill.*

He looked around, thinking it was good country for game. *A great place for a base camp during hunting season. I'll scout the area tomorrow, maybe find a trail to run, and keep my eyes open for deer and elk.* In a couple of weeks, he and his dad, along with Steve Peterson and his dad, Orlo, would come there to hunt.

A hundred yards to his left, a narrow gorge opened to the valley. It was from the gorge that the little stream flowed. The gorge looked secluded, wild. *I bet there's a lot of wildlife in that gully*, Tommy mused. *I have a feeling some animal is watching me right now.* It was just a vague feeling. He saw no furtive movement, no stirring of brush, no moving shadow. Nor did he hear anything unusual. It was nothing to worry about, anyway.

Tommy explored the mountainside just above the valley floor, and, as he had expected, he found a game trail, switchbacking down the mountain. Deer, elk, bears, maybe even cougars, came off the mountain to drink from the stream, or to graze the meadow. *Good. I'll run that trail tomorrow. See where it goes.* Tommy was pleased. So far, his cleansing run was working out just fine.

Satisfied, he returned to where he had left his pack. He chose a place to sleep, then sat down to eat a package of trail mix. He still had a sensation of being watched. *Why would I feel that way?* Tommy wondered. *And why should I worry about it? Wild animals watch us all the time, and we don't even know it. But what if it isn't an animal? What if it's a person? A wild man?* He laughed at the thought, and went to sleep.

8. LITTLE BEAR

Tommy woke up early, feeling refreshed. The night, he mused, had been uneventful, after all. He yawned, stretched, sat up, and then leaped to his feet. Ten feet away, a black dog rested on its belly, facing him. The dog's bright brown eyes watched Tommy intently.

Tommy caught his breath, relaxed and smiled. "Hello, dog," he said. "So it was you watching me yesterday." He held out a hand, but the dog did not move. Didn't even blink. Tommy took a step to get out of the shelter, and the dog immediately rose to its feet and backed up a few steps. Those sharp eyes followed Tommy's every move.

"Wild, are you?" The dog looked ready to run. "You've been lost for a while. Been chased a time or two. Well, I have something I think you'll like." Tommy rummaged in his pack and found the package of beef jerky. He took out a strip and offered it to the dog. "Here you go," he said, quietly.

The wary dog did not move.

"Okay," Tommy said. He tossed the meat to the dog, a little bit to the side. It turned its head and sniffed, still without taking its eyes off Tommy. Then the hungry dog snatched up the jerky and swallowed it in one gulp.

Tommy laughed. "I thought so. You're hungry. I wish I had more to give you, but I'm traveling on short rations. I didn't expect to have company."

That's a good looking dog, Tommy mused. *Part Border Collie, some Heeler. Who knows what else? Probably thin under all that hair, but he looks strong, and healthy.* Tommy appraised the medium sized, long haired dog, black with some tan around the eyes and a spot of white on the chest. Short floppy ears.

"I'm glad I didn't run into you in the dark," Tommy commented. "I might have mistaken you for a bear. A little bear, but they're bad trouble if momma bear is somewhere close. Hey, I'll call you Little Bear."

What would the dog do? he wondered. He planned to run that game trail. Would the dog stay with him? He wished he had something else to feed the poor animal. But he hadn't come to hunt. Didn't have a gun with him.

"I'll take you back with me, try to find a good home for you. Until then, we're gonna have to tough it out." Sitting motionless, the dog watched as Tommy stuffed his meager supplies in his pack and closed it. He picked it up, shouldered it, and asked, "Are you coming, Little Bear?" He turned toward the trail he wanted to explore, walked a few steps, and looked back. Tail happily waving, Little Bear padded along a few steps behind him.

Tommy had always had a dog. But when the collie he'd grown up with died, he didn't want a replacement, not right away. Then he got busy in school, and with the wild horse, and thought no more about a dog. Now he wondered if there was any significance in the fact that he'd found this dog, or the dog had found him, in the very place where he had caught the shadow horse. Or was it merely a coincidence?

Tommy's grandfather didn't believe in coincidences. "Everything happens for a reason," he declared, "and with the passing of time, the reasons will reveal themselves." *Well*, Tommy decided, *that's good enough for me*. He looked back and was pleased to see the shaggy dog, still following.

Tommy jogged and hiked up the trail, looking for, and finding, evidence of deer and elk in the area. *A real nice place, and it'll be good hunting*, he thought. Occupied with his thoughts, he went a couple of hours before stopping. It was easy going; the animals never went straight up or down a mountain. With plenty of time in their lives, they always found the easiest way.

When he came to the crest of a little ridge, Tommy stopped, and said, "I'm gonna take my bearings, Little Bear. There may be snow in those clouds. If we get snow, this will look a lot different when we come back tomorrow." Little Bear sat patiently while Tommy took a compass reading on a snag, an old, dead tree, still standing, that would be easy to see. A good reference point.

It began to snow within the hour, and when Tommy saw a small spring he stopped. "We better stay here tonight, Bear," he said. "No telling how far we might have to go before we find more water. And it'll be dark soon."

The spring was no more than a seep with running water, actually. Now Tommy drank directly from the spring; there were no beavers at that altitude. Beavers needed more water, and different trees, like aspen and willow, for food and for building their dams and houses. The water was so cold Tommy had to sip slowly. Little Bear sat, politely waiting. When Tommy got up and stepped back, Bear took his turn.

Watching Little Bear drink, Tommy studied the small spring and marveled at nature's wonderful ways. A mountain squirrel had stored fir and pine cones in the spring, and, in his mind's eye, Tommy visualized the squirrel bringing one cone at a time, placing it just so, then patting it down with its front feet. In precise rows, the cones might have been put there by an engineer. The bottom of the little spring was solidly lined. The cold water kept the cones from opening and losing their seeds, and the running water would never freeze.

Tommy knew the little squirrel had stored many more cones under rocks, or logs, sometimes just in a depression in the ground. If the snow got too deep for him to get at those cones, he could get one from his emergency supply in the spring.

Tommy looked around and saw an old tree that had been downed in a long-ago storm. It rested horizontally, three or four feet off the ground, on the stubs of broken off branches. *That's perfect,* Tommy thought. *It'll make a great shelter, with a little work.*

He leaned stout sticks against the log, on the uphill side. Those he covered with pine boughs to make a tight roof that, collecting snow, would give complete protection from the weather.

Tommy stood back, pleased with his creation. Then he prepared a fireplace, just in case, and gathered an armful of dry wood, which he piled just inside the shelter. "Now," he said, "Let it snow. Hey, Bear, it's supper time."

He held out a strip of jerky, wondering if the wary dog would take it from his hand. But Little Bear, who most certainly was desperately hungry, would not. Again, Tommy put the meat on the ground. He did not toss it, just laid it down. Bear crept closer and snatched up the jerky.

"There you go, Bear," Tommy said. "It's not much, but it's all I can spare for now. Like I said, we're toughing it out on this trip."

Would the dog stay with him another day? Two more days? Or would hunger make him leave? Tommy realized how much he had come to like the half-wild dog.

The snow came thicker and began accumulating on the ground. It clung to everything in the mild temperature, making a snow house out of Tommy's shelter. "It's beautiful, Bear," Tommy said. "There's nothing better than a good snowstorm."

Already wearing his jacket, stocking cap and gloves, Tommy got into his shelter and wrapped himself in his survival blanket. He lay down and called, "Come on, Bear. Come inside." Little Bear did not move, but he whined, just audibly. "Good dog," Tommy said. He turned his back and waited quietly. Then, cautiously and ever so slowly, Little Bear crept into the shelter. He turned around twice, then lay down against Tommy's back. Tommy smiled.

There was not a sound when Tommy woke up at daylight. It had snowed all night, was still coming down heavily. *Looks like it's a foot deep, at least,* Tommy thought. The thick white blanket covered everything, softened the contours of the land. "Man, that's beautiful," Tommy muttered. Then he stiffened, looked around, and said, "Hey, wait a minute! Where's Little Bear?"

The dog was nowhere to be seen. Nor were there any tracks. *He's been gone a while. His tracks are filled with snow.* Tommy was puzzled.

Was the dog hunting? Had he finally given up and left to try to find his way down the mountain? A shiver raced through Tommy's body. Could Little Bear make it out, if that was what he was trying to do? *Did I make a mistake? Should I have given the dog the last few strips of jerky? No*, Tommy thought, *I did what I thought best.*

The dog's absence put a damper on Tommy's enjoyment of the first snowstorm of the winter. He plodded dejectedly to the spring, not caring that his running shoes filled with snow, soaking his feet. *No problem*, he mused, *I have to start for home today, anyway. I'll be walking in snow. But it's warm. My feet will be okay as long as I keep going. And I think I'll run out of snow lower down, anyway.*

Back in his shelter, Tommy ate trail mix and wondered if he might as well eat a strip of jerky. He decided not to, knowing that if Little Bear did come back, he would feel terrible about not having saved it.

When he had finished, he stuffed his few belongings in his pack, crawled out of the shelter, and stood for a few minutes. Without admitting it to himself, he looked for a mound of snow that didn't belong there. He did not want to think that perhaps the dog simply died during the night, was lying out there under a blanket of snow.

Tommy looked up and saw a little black dot. Moving. As he watched, heart thumping, the dot came closer, grew larger, and became Little Bear. The dog carried something.

"Little Bear!" Tommy called, excited. "What did you find?" At the sound of Tommy's voice, Little Bear began plunging through the snow to where Tommy stood, and dropped his burden at Tommy's feet. Wagging his tail, he looked up proudly.

"A grouse!" Tommy exclaimed. "You found a grouse!" It was one of those strange birds, sometimes called prairie chicken. They were pretty good flyers, but spent a lot of time on the ground, feeding on seeds, berries, insects, or anything they could find. They nested on the ground. *This one must have been huddling under a clump of sage, waiting out the storm.* Or was it something long dead? He picked it up. The bird was still soft, even a little bit warm. Blood dripped from a bite wound on the neck. The bird was freshly killed!

Tommy looked into Little Bear's sparkling eyes and said, "You could have eaten it, but you brought it to me. You're something else, Little Bear."

Tommy lit the already prepared fire and began plucking the grouse. With just his hands and pocket knife, he did a very poor job of cleaning the bird. But it didn't matter; this was a special occasion. An early Thanksgiving.

Tommy cooked the grouse on a stick. When he thought it was done enough, he cut off a very small piece for himself and gave the rest to Little Bear. The hungry dog devoured the bird speedily, bones and all. Tommy shook his head. *That poor dog was starving*, he mused.

When he was certain his fire was out, Tommy shouldered his pack and said, "Let's go home, Bear." He started down the trail, plodded several steps through knee-deep snow, and heard Little Bear growling. He stopped and looked back. "What is it, Bear?" The dog stood stiffly, looking up the trail, growling low.

9. THE PHANTOM HORSE

At first, Tommy couldn't see anything but falling snow. He waited, and soon he heard muffled, rhythmic thumping. Something was coming down the trail. Something big. Then, a large, dark form took shape, ghostlike, coming out of the curtain of snow. Little Bear woofed.

Tommy laughed. "Hey," he exclaimed, "it's a horse! All by himself. It's okay, Bear. Somebody's horse got loose." Four feet of rope, frayed at the end, hung from the horse's halter.

The big horse walked past Little Bear, who had to back out of the way to keep from getting stepped on. The horse stopped when Tommy reached out to grab the dangling rope.

"Hello, horse. Where did you come from?" Tommy asked. "What happened? You had to pull pretty hard to break this rope."

Holding the broken rope loosely, Tommy stroked the big horse's neck. Taut muscles quivered under his touch, yet the horse eyed Tommy with a look of trust. *A gentle horse*, Tommy mused, *But something happened to make him break his halter rope.* Tommy walked around to the off side of the horse and sucked in his breath. Two sets of parallel claw marks gouged the horse's hide from the withers back almost to the hip. Wet blood still seeped from the shoulder wounds.

"Oh, man!" Tommy exclaimed. "A cougar jumped you! No wonder you broke your rope, and it's a good thing you did."

But what about the horse's rider? There was at least one person still somewhere up on the mountain. Was that person hurt? Dead? *Somebody is afoot, if nothing else.*

"Little Bear," Tommy said, "We have to go back up the trail and find out if somebody needs help. I hope this horse will let me ride him."

He led the horse over to one of the snow-covered mounds which he knew was a boulder. He brushed off the snow, parked the horse close, and eased himself very carefully onto the big horse's back. The horse flinched a little when Tommy's right leg touched the off side, then stood quietly.

"Good boy," Tommy said, petting the horse on the neck. He sat quietly for a moment. Would the injured horse tolerate a rider? *Have to give it a try. I can't see myself hiking up that trail. Not in this snow.* With gentle pressure of the halter rope against the horse's neck, and a bit of leg pressure on the uninjured near side, Tommy asked the horse to move. Obediently, the big horse turned and began walking back up the trail.

Tommy patted the horse on the neck. "You can go through the deep snow easier than I can," Tommy told him. "I'll be warm, riding bareback, and I need to save my energy."

Wearing clothes far more suitable for hiking and jogging, with a total of two packages of trail mix and a couple of strips of beef jerky, he and Little Bear were poorly prepared for this uncertain new adventure. Even with the horse, was he being foolish? Ought he, instead, ride down the mountain and send professionals up here? He didn't know. But he did know that time might be the most important factor. There was no choice, really. "Coming, Bear?" he called. He looked behind him and saw Little Bear following in the tall horse's tracks.

It had stopped snowing by then. Tommy could see the tracks the horse had made coming down, so he knew he was okay. In addition, the horse was a good walker, and seemed to know where he was going.

As the day wore on Tommy couldn't help worrying about how far he had to go to get to the hunter's camp. Had the horse been walking all night before getting to Tommy's camp? He had been plodding for several hours. "You're a good mountain horse," Tommy said. "I'm glad I didn't have to hike all this way in the snow." He was, in fact, beginning to get tired. *Couldn't make it without the horse. I sure hope we find some water. I bet this horse is thirsty, too.* He saw Little Bear grabbing a mouthful of snow from time to time.

Was there no end to this journey? How much farther could the good horse go without stopping?

We've been on the trail for what, six or seven hours? Had he made a big mistake? *Maybe*, he thought. *But I've come this far. It's too late now to change my mind.* And then, was it his imagination? The big horse, that must be getting tired, seemed to be walking faster. As though hurrying. And then suddenly, apparently in the middle of nowhere, the horse simply stopped.

In the dim light of a cloudy, late afternoon, all Tommy could see was snow, and more snow. Then he noticed a mound of snow that might have a tent under it. "Hello! Is anybody here?" he shouted.

Tommy heard nothing, but Little Bear woofed. Tommy saw the dog standing listening, staring intently off to the side.

Tommy slid off the horse, tied him loosely to a small tree, and went to Little Bear. From there, he began walking in the direction the dog seemed to be looking. He called again, and this time heard a reply, sounding like it was far away. "Down here, in the gully," a man called out.

"Okay, I'm coming," Tommy answered. The warning came back quickly. "Don't come too close, or you'll fall in here like I did."

10. RESCUE

Tommy tested the slippery ground with every step. When he felt the slope grow steeper, he stopped, grabbed a tree, and called out, "Are you all right down there?"

"I'm okay. But I can't climb out. Have you got a rope?"

"No."

"There's a rope on my saddle. It's hanging on a tree close to my tent."

"All right, I'll get it." Tommy went back to the camp site and brushed the snow off what he had thought was a tent. It was, for a fact, a tent. And close by, also covered with snow, he saw the saddle. A well-worn nylon lariat, about thirty-five feet long, hung from the saddle.

Good. But I know I can't pull a man out of the gully. And this old nylon rope is slick. He'll never be able to climb it. I need to use the horse. He's probably and old ranch horse. He'll know how to work a rope.

But those claw marks scare me. Little Bear sat, quietly watching.

"How about it, old horse?" Tommy asked as he examined the scratches. "We have to get your man out of that gully. You're our only hope. You didn't fuss about my leg on your side, but a tight saddle and a hard pull on a rope is a whole different story. I wish I had more padding." All he had, besides the saddle blanket, was his survival blanket, and it was no padding at all. Then he smiled, and said, "Little Bear, that man has to have a bedroll. Let's go see."

With Bear following, Tommy went to the tent, went in and felt his way around in the dark. He found a sleeping bag, reached inside, and pulled out a thick, wool blanket.

"This is just what we need, Bear." Tommy felt a surge of excitement.

He folded the blanket twice and laid it over the horse's back so it covered the clawed scratches. He put the regular saddle pad over the blanket, and then the heavy saddle. He went around to the off side, made sure there were no wrinkles, then pulled up the cinch, just snug, and said, "There, now let's give it a minute to warm your back."

Tommy was pleased to see a snaffle bit in the bridle. It meant the horse was easy to handle.

Tommy bridled the horse, fitted the breast collar, and tightened the cinch. Then he led the horse a few steps to see what would happen. The horse was calm, and Tommy stepped into the saddle. Again, the horse remained quiet. "Good, real good," Tommy said, patting the horse on the neck. "Now let's try the rope."

He shook out a loop, tossed it over a dead, broken branch, and asked the horse to pull. The tall horse pulled the rope tight, and the branch broke off. Again, Tommy praised the horse. "Okay, let's go," he said. "Are you coming, Bear?"

He rode as close to the gully as he dared and called down, "Hey, I've got the rope. And I brought the horse. If he'll do it, he can pull you up."

"Yeah, good. He's been a rope horse."

"Okay. I'll toss you some rope when you're ready."

"Throw it down."

Tommy tossed the rope, and the man said, "Got it! Give me a minute to tie it around me." While he waited, Tommy got off and tightened the cinch another notch. "Sorry about that," he said to the horse. "We don't want the saddle to slip. Not even a little bit."

"Okay, I'm ready," the man called from the gully. "Let's try it. But this is going to be hard. Take it slow."

Back in the saddle, Tommy pulled up the slack and took a dally. "Here we go!" he said. He moved the horse a few steps, and the rope went tight. Real tight. "Okay down there?" he asked.

"Yeah. But these rocks are slick. Take it easy!"

It was a hard pull. Besides the weight of the man, there was friction where the rope slid over the edge of the gully. The horse lowered his head and dug in. Then, to add to the difficulty, his feet began to slip on the wet ground. To rest the horse, and the man, Tommy stopped again.

"How's it going?" he called.

"Good. Pull me up."

The saddle had a slick horn, not made for dallying. The smooth lariat slipped, little by little. He couldn't hold it with one hand. He took another quick wrap, wondering if he should have tied hard and fast. *No, no!* he thought. *This is the only way. If the horse begins to hurt, he might blow up. If he thinks the big cat is on his back again he'll run off, or buck or something. I have to be able to let go if that happens. If I tied hard and fast, the horse might drag the man to death.*

The horse was sweating, and he began to fret. He switched his tail, pinned his ears back, and tugged at the bit. Tommy leaned forward, spoke softly. "Easy boy. Easy does it." He gave little tugs on the bit to distract the horse. *Isn't that man out of the gully yet?* he wondered.

This horse is gonna blow. I'll have to bail out, real fast, and try to grab a tree and take a wrap so that man that doesn't fall back into the gully. I just hope I can do it!

Suddenly the big horse bowed his neck, dropped his head, and nearly yanked the reins out of Tommy's left hand. In desperation, he let the right rein slip, wrapped the left rein around his hand with a quick twist of his wrist, and pulled back as hard as he could. He dragged his horse's head around and back to his knee. It gave him momentary control.

"Whoa, boy! Whoa now," he said while he prepared to jump off. Then he heard a shout, "I'm out!"

Quickly, Tommy unwound his dally and dismounted. He held the rope in his right hand and the bridle rein in his left, while the big horse danced around.

"Are you up? Are you okay?" Tommy called.

"Yes, you can drop the rope."

Tommy dropped the rope, grabbed the horse's bridle with his left hand, gave the latigo a quick tug and unbuckled the cinch. The sweating, trembling horse calmed down as Tommy soothed him with voice and hands.

Tommy led the horse toward where the rescued man stood. His legs shook, and he discovered that he was drenched with sweat. *Man*, he thought, *I'm played out. I couldn't have lasted much longer*. He saw the sturdily-built man carefully coiling the lariat, and all the nervous tension drained out of him.

The rescued man wore hunting camouflage. Insulated pants and jacket, expensive boots, and an orange cap with earflaps. Tommy smiled to himself, thinking, *He knows how to dress for the mountains. I wonder what he'll think of me, in my running shoes and clothes.*

When Tommy walked up, the man smiled, held out his hand, and said, "My name's John Hanson. I'm indebted to you. How did you find me?"

"Kind of by accident. It's a long story. Basically, your horse brought me here. I'm Tommy Lewis. Are you okay?"

"Yeah, I'm okay. Got a few little sprains and bruises, tore up my clothes. But I'm lucky; it could have been a lot worse. Hey, let's get up to camp. I'm beat, and you look cold. You're shivering."

A nice guy, Tommy mused as they walked to the campsite. *And he's tough. He must have been in that gully all last night and all day today.* When they got to the camp, Tommy said, "I'll take care of Old Faithful here. Do you have something to feed him?"

"There should be a sack of alfalfa cubes, if the animals haven't dragged it away. It'll be under that tarp, where you found the saddle." He walked a few steps, then stopped, and said, "Old Faithful. That's a good name. I call him Smokestack. Old Smokey, for short."

Tommy grinned, and said, "Well, he's black, and he's tall."

"Been a good horse."

"He's a good one, all right. Did you know what happened to him?"

"No. I heard a commotion last night, but I was in the gully and didn't know what was going on."

"Look here," Tommy said. He turned the horse around, and pointed to his shoulder. He had unsaddled while they talked. Hanson ran his hand over the tall horse's side, and exclaimed, "My God! A mountain lion jumped him! And he broke loose. I'm lucky he didn't come after me. I didn't have a gun. But I guess lions don't like to eat people."

"No, they don't. Only if they're starving. They fear people, but they like horses best of all."

Then Tommy held out the wool blanket, and said, "Here. This is yours. I swiped it out of your sleeping bag. I thought I needed some extra padding. I didn't say anything about it before, because I thought you already had enough to worry about."

Hanson stared at Tommy. "You did exactly right," he said. "That's good thinking. This gets more interesting all the time. I want to hear all about it. But first let's get done here and go to the tent. I'll dig out the feed sack while you take Old Faithful to water. The spring's over there, under that big fir tree."

With Little Bear trailing, Tommy led the horse to the spring. Although he was shivering with cold, Tommy took a long drink from the spring. He hadn't had anything to eat or drink since early morning. Dehydration was as serious a threat as hypothermia, and he knew he would get in the tent in a few minutes.

Hanson had found the alfalfa cubes, and he held out an old turnout blanket. "Let's put this on him."

"Good idea. Is he broke to hobbles?"

"Yes, he is."

"This halter shank is too short now. I'll use it to make hobbles."

"Yeah, that's good. I'll go to the tent and get us something to eat."

Tommy put the makeshift hobbles on the big horse. He scraped the snow away, made a small spot on the ground to feed the horse, and poured out half of what was left of the hay cubes. "There you go, boy," he said. "I'll give you the rest in the morning." He fastened the buckles and snaps on the turnout blanket, and said, "You're all set. Little Bear will let us know if another cougar, or a bear, comes around." He gave the horse an affectionate pat on the rump and started for the tent.

11.TWO OF A KIND

"Man, that smells good!" Tommy exclaimed as he entered the tent. Hanson was tending a small pot on a little propane camp stove.

"Canned bacon and beans warming up," Hanson replied. "It's not much, but all I have. There's enough for both of us, and more of the same for breakfast, then that's it. I thought I'd be home by now."

"It'll be a real treat for me," Tommy declared.

"Well, here you go," Hanson handed Tommy a full dish. There was no more talk for a while, and then Tommy said, "You had a bad fall. Lucky you didn't break something."

"Yes. I was tracking an elk. It was snowing, getting dark. Everything looked the same. I couldn't tell up from down. Didn't realize I was so close to the gully until I began to slip. My feet went out from under me and down I went."

"And there's no way out?"

"Not that I could see. I walked pretty far up the gully this morning. Couldn't climb out anywhere. I thought I was going to have to wait for the snow to melt."

Hanson wiped the empty plates with a paper towel. He started heating water for coffee, and eyed Tommy. Body heat and the little propane burner had warmed the tent, and Tommy shed his jacket and stocking cap. His braids dropped, and Hanson smiled.

"I thought I knew that name," he said. "It was you who caught the wild stallion, and then, just last Labor Day, found a herd of stolen cattle. I saw it on TV."

"Yes, that was me," Tommy admitted. "Something happens, and the reporters make a big deal out of it."

"Maybe so, but those were good stories." Hanson was quiet for a minute, then said, "And here you are. What I want to know is how you found me."

Tommy told Hanson about the cleansing run, and how Old Faithful came down the trail that morning. "He came and got me, and brought me back to your camp," Tommy laughed.

"It's a miracle," Hanson said, frowning. "I made a mistake, coming up here alone. There were three of us, but one man got sick, and somebody had to go back with him. I stayed. Bad idea, wasn't it?"

"What can I say? I'm alone, too."

"I guess that makes us two of a kind," Hanson sipped his coffee, then observed, "It's a whole lot of coincidences isn't it?"

147

"My grandfather doesn't believe in luck. He says that everything happens for a reason."

"Yes, I know that philosophy. And I like it. Well, whatever you want to call it, I owe you, big time. But hey, let's get some sleep. Want to bring your dog in here?"

"I don't know if he's my dog. He was pretty wild when I found him. I don't know if he'll come inside." Tommy barely got the door flap opened when Little Bear bounded in and began licking Tommy's face.

Hanson laughed, and said, "He's your dog, all right."

"Are you going to walk down the mountain wearing those shoes?" Hanson asked. They were packing, the next morning, for the trip home.

"Sure," Tommy replied. "My feet will be wet, but they'll stay warm as long as I'm walking. And I think we'll run out of snow lower down."

Hanson shook his head skeptically. He borrowed Tommy's idea of providing extra padding under his saddle, and used the folded blanket as Tommy had. They were in good spirits when they started down the trail. A mild temperature and the warming sun made it seem like a spring day. The tall horse strode briskly down the trail, and Tommy grinned at the sight of Little Bear's proudly waving tail as the dog followed in the horse's path through the snow.

As Tommy had thought, there was less and less snow the farther down they went. When the snow dwindled to a mere inch or so, Tommy took the lead. He jogged most of the way from there on, and Old Faithful had to trot occasionally to keep up.

Tommy set a pace that took them to the little valley, where he had spent his first night, a little after noon. There was no snow there at all. Old Faithful grazed while Tommy and Hanson rested.

Tommy told Hanson about catching the shadow horse there the previous summer, and then finding Little Bear in the same place a few days ago. "Another coincidence," Tommy grinned. "Dad and I, and two friends, will make this our base camp when we come up here to hunt in a couple of weeks."

"Couldn't find a better spot," Hanson commented. "Good grass and water for the horses, and we know there's game here."

They didn't linger. The urge to get down the mountain made them eager to be on their way. Again, Tommy led the way, walking and jogging alternately. It took less than an hour to get to the beaver pond.

"Do you want to stop here, finish the trip tomorrow?" Hanson asked. "You must be pretty tired."

"Well, I have to admit I'm a little bit tired. But I want to go on home. How's Old Faithful doing?"

"He seems okay. The extra blanket helps, I'm sure of that."

"Okay. I'll eat my last package of trail mix and give Bear the last strip of jerky, and that'll get us home. It's all downhill from here."

When it got dark, Al Lewis kept going to the door and looking toward the mountain. He was sure Tommy would get home that evening. And finally,

149

after several such trips, Al thought he heard a horse walking. He stepped outside and waited, listening, and in a few minutes they came out of the dark. Tommy was walking, and behind him there was someone on a horse. When they got closer, Al saw the dog. "Hi, Tommy!" he called.

Tommy jogged up and stopped. Hanson dismounted, and Tommy said, "Dad, this is Mr. Hanson."

They shook hands, and Hanson said, "Name's John."

"Well, John," Al Lewis said, "if you're a friend of Tommy's, you're a friend of the family. You're welcome to stay the night."

"I hadn't planned on it. I just wanted to make sure Tommy got home okay. I can call my friend, he'll pick me up. He'll bring a trailer."

"Okay, you can do that. But I think you should stay here tonight. You guys look beat."

"I don't want to be any trouble," Hanson said. "But I just might do that. I have my camping gear, and can sleep in the barn."

"You'll sleep in our spare bedroom. Tommy, let's put the horse in the little corral behind the barn. Give him some hay. There's water in the tank."

When they went to the house, Betty Lewis took one look and said, "You look like you're starving. I'll see what I can find while you wash up."

She put soup, sandwiches, milk and coffee on the table. While they ate, Hanson told them about his fall into the gully and subsequent rescue. "I wanted to see you so I could tell you what Tommy did. I'll never be able to thank him enough."

Tommy grinned self-consciously, and said, "Well, things just kept happening. The cougar started it. Old Faithful broke his halter rope and came down the trail."

"Yes," Hanson said, "but you read the signs and knew what to do. You knew you were taking a chance, going up the trail like that. I've been on some search and rescue missions, and I know how important every little thing is." He saw the curious looks directed his way, and said, "I'm a deputy sheriff in Garfield County. I live in Rifle."

"I've been up that way a time or two, on fires," Al Lewis said.

"Tommy told me you work for the forest service. You can be proud of him. I have to say, pulling me out of the gully with an injured horse took a whole lot of doing. Don't know how he did it, really. He's good with horses, for sure."

"Yes, we're proud of him," Al Lewis replied. "We just don't know how he manages to find all these adventures. He's become a celebrity."

"Tommy mentioned that. Said the publicity got tiresome, after while." Then he smiled, and said, "Let me guess. I think maybe all of you would like to keep this little episode quiet. At least for now."

"How about it, Son?"

"Yes, I think so," Tommy replied.

"Okay. It'll be our secret. Besides, they'd think I'm telling a big windy, back home. I have to admit it's kind of unbelievable. There'll be the cougar scars to explain, but I'll think of something."

"John, are you going to hunt in the rifle season?" Al Lewis inquired.

"I planned to."

"You can hunt with us, unless you have other arrangements. We'd like to have you. It's only a couple of weeks away. You can leave your horse here in the meantime."

"Well, thanks," Hanson replied. "Yeah, I'd like to do that. Sounds great."

12. GOING FISHING

It had been a good winter for Tommy. True to his word, Deputy Sheriff John Hanson never reported his fall into a gully and subsequent rescue. Classmates forgot about teasing Tommy, the hero, and he enjoyed being just another student in high school.

During summer vacations, Tommy found work, and pleasure, helping Steve and his dad, Orlo Peterson, who had a large ranch and a herd of cattle. His own father had a small place, and worked full time for the forest service. Steve, now fourteen years old, was a competent ranch hand. He was growing, would be a big man, like his father. Now school was out, and the boys had been working hard.

Calves had been branded and doctored, the cattle moved to summer pasture on forest service land. Tommy and Steve hauled and stacked Orlo's first cutting of hay, while Orlo ran the baler. When the last bale was stacked, Orlo said, "That's enough work for a while. You boys should take some time off. Go fishing, or something."

"That's a good idea!" Steve exclaimed. "How about it, Tommy?"

"Sounds good to me."

"Take a week, at least," Orlo suggested. "I'll check the cattle while you're gone. Old Rawhide's getting fat; he needs exercise." Rawhide was Orlo's personal saddle horse; a big, strong horse for a big, strong man.

The boys started their trip early the next morning. Steve rode Diamond Lil, Tommy rode Shadow, and Little Bear scouted ahead. They went up the Little Porcupine Creek trail to get to the high country. Once, when a marmot's piercing whistle sounded from almost underfoot, Little Bear jumped back. Then he charged.

Tommy laughed, and said, "You're lucky that marmot went to his hole, Bear. He'd have given you a real fight if you'd have caught him." Little Bear pranced up the trail; he had done his job.

They had decided to go to the Shepherds Lake Campground, about thirty miles north, according to Tommy's White River National Forest topographical map. By mid-afternoon, even with a stop for a sandwich, they figured they were more than half way to the lake.

Enjoying their ride, and the beautiful day, Steve and Tommy were unaware, at first, that the thud of their horse's feet on the hard-packed trail had grown quiet. When Tommy noticed, he looked down, and said, "Hey, Steve, look at that!" The trail had been churned up by the hooves of many horses.

"Man, I hope all those dudes aren't going to Shepherds Lake," Steve said. "What do you suppose it is, a big trail ride?"

"Well, who knows? But look, those horses are barefoot. Trail riders would be riding shod horses."

"Could they be mustangs? Wild horses?"

"Maybe. But I haven't heard about any BLM roundup."

"Look there," Steve said, pointing down at the trail. "There's a footprint made by a horse wearing shoes."

They stopped their horses and got off for a better look. The circular, smooth print definitely was that of a horseshoe.

"It looks like somebody is herding those horses," Tommy observed. They rode on, watching and wondering. Suddenly Tommy stopped his horse, jumped off, and knelt beside the trail. "Look here, Steve," he exclaimed. "What do you make of this?"

Steve got down, studied the tracks Tommy indicated, and said, "I think one horse tried to run off, and somebody went after it. But there's something funny about those tracks."

"I'll say there is," Tommy replied. "That horse was traveling on three legs."

"On three legs?"

"Yes. It's an old mustangers' trick. They fold a foreleg back at the knee and tie it that way. Makes a troublesome horse easier to handle."

"That's terrible! Doesn't that cripple a horse?"

"It does if the leg is kept tied up too long. But the mustangers don't care; they sell the horses for slaughter, anyway. That tells me somebody is stealing horses. No one with a BLM permit to gather wild horses would be permitted to do that. They wouldn't even want to."

"Man, we ought to try to do something about this! What can we do?"

"We can report it to the BLM, or the forest service."

"We'll have to go all the way back to Rifle Gap Park."

"Maybe not," Tommy said. "Let's see." He got his map, spread it out on the ground, and asked, "Did you see this little trail branching off to the east a mile or so back?"

"Yeah, I saw it."

"Well, look. It goes to Lost Lake. Looks like it's only about four or five miles. And there's a road going to the lake. There may be a ranger there, or at least a telephone."

"An hour's ride. Let's go."

"Can you do it?" Tommy asked. He pointed north, and said, "Those are storm clouds. A hard rain will wash out the tracks. Maybe I should follow the horses, so we don't lose them."

"Yeah, you're right. Sure, I'll go."

"Okay," Tommy said. "But first, let's rearrange our packs, so we each have some food, and something to cook with. You keep the tent."

157

"Okay, good idea," Steve replied. Then he joked, "I may never see you again. But hey, where will we meet?"

"Let's make it Shepherds Lake. We're going there, anyway."

Steve nodded, mounted Diamond Lil, and said, "You be careful, hear? Don't get yourself shot!" Tommy laughed and waved him off. Then he mounted and started north, with Little Bear scouting up front.

The storm clouds got blacker, came closer, and a scatter of wind-driven rain persuaded Tommy to put on his slicker.

Soon the rain became a downpour, and turned the trail into a sea of mud. Shadow plodded, splashing, and Little Bear trotted along behind, head and trail drooping.

With his head down against the pelting rain, Tommy almost missed seeing where the mustangs left the trail and went west, into a series of wooded hills.

I bet those guys are looking for a place to lay over for a day or two. With the rain washing out their tracks, they'll feel safe, hiding in the hills.

Tommy held Shadow to a slow walk, and kept a sharp eye on the terrain ahead. He had gone nearly all the way around the first hill when Shadow raised his head and perked up his ears. "Whoa, Shadow," Tommy said, softly. "What are you looking at?"

He stopped, turned around and rode back about fifty yards. He tied Shadow to a tree, and shed his slicker. It had almost stopped raining by then, and the slicker was too cumbersome, too visible, and made too much noise for sneaking through the woods.

Tommy and Little Bear crept cautiously around the hillside. A few steps beyond where he had stopped, Tommy saw the horses through the thinning trees below him.

Man, he thought, *there must be fifty horses there*! It was a wonderful sight, except that they were being stolen, and would be sold for dog food.

The mustangs grazed on level ground below the hill. Tired from a long drive, they eagerly cropped the lush grass. Two riders watched the herd. *I think they'll stay here a day or two. I'll go back, go to Shepherds Lake, and wait for Steve. Man, this is working out good*.

He turned to go back, and Little Bear growled. Tommy put his hand on Bear's head, and whispered, "Quiet, Bear."

He had taken just one step, then stopped in mid-stride when a harsh voice called out, "Hold it, mister!"

13 CAPTURED

Tommy raised his hands above his head. "Easy, Bear," he cautioned the growling dog. He looked back and saw a thin, bearded man carrying a carbine. The man was limping. *Adam! The rustler Shadow ran over last fall at the canyon*! Quickly, Tommy turned away. Had Adam recognized him?

"What'cha doin' here?"

"I'm on my way to Shepherds Lake." Tommy attempted to disguise his voice.

"You alone?"

"Yes."

"Where's your horse?"

"No horse. I'm hiking."

"Not with them boots, you ain't." Adam spat. "Git goin', we'll see about the horse."

Disturbed by Adam's quarrelsome voice, Shadow shuffled around nervously. Adam spotted the movement through the trees, and said, "Yep, there's your horse." He was quiet for a minute, then blurted,

161

"Hold on! I know you! Turn around!" Harsh, double metallic clicks warned Tommy that a round had been chambered in Adam's rifle, and the gun cocked. It was ready to fire with just an easy pull on the trigger. With all hope lost, Tommy turned to face the rustler.

"Sure!" Adam exclaimed. "You're the Indian kid who ran your horse over me last fall. Wrecked my hip! I'm gonna settle that score." He turned sideways, braced himself, and brought his gun to his shoulder. Then a voice rang out, "No, Adam! No gunshots! We're too close to the campground. We'll take care of the kid later."

Tommy knew that voice! Knew it well! He watched in disbelief as Mexico Bill rode up on a chestnut Quarter Horse gelding. "No gunshots," he repeated. Adam held steady for a minute, then spat, swore, and lowered his gun.

Mexico Bill, my old friend, a mustanger? Impossible! Not the man who had helped him train the shadow horse, the man with whom he had traveled to rodeos, where Bill did his fancy roping, and Tommy performed his "Indian" act with Shadow? Certainly not Mexico Bill!

Adam swore, and said, "All right. But I'm gonna take that horse."

He'll get a surprise if he tries to ride Shadow. I hope he does. I might get out of this after all.

But Bill said, "No. Leave the horse. Too many people have seen him. Even on TV. Somebody will put two and two together. We can't take that chance. You take the kid down to camp. I'll get rid of the horse." He looked Tommy in the eye, held the look for a moment, and said, "And the dog. I'll take care of the dog, too."

Tommy was confused. Was there a message in that look? Would Bill kill Little Bear? Adam would, for sure. Tommy leaned down, put a hand on the trembling dog pressing against his leg and said, quietly, "Go, Bear." He gave the dog a little shove.

"All right, let's go," Adam said. He motioned with the gun for Tommy to go down the hill.

Tommy trudged dejectedly, shaking with fear. Could he whirl, strike the rifle aside, and tackle Adam? He glanced back. It wouldn't work. *Adam's too smart for that. He's keeping his distance. He would like for me to give him an excuse to shoot me. I might get a bullet in the back anyway, in spite of Bill's warning. Adam'll claim I tried to run off, even if I don't.*

Tommy went on down the hill, wondering if he would ever see his parents again. He wondered, too, if Bill would kill Shadow and Little Bear. He had heard no gunshots, but that didn't mean anything. There were other ways to kill an animal. Or a person. Tommy pictured Bill's big, sharp hunting knife and shuddered. He walked down the hill, drained of energy, with all hope lost.

He saw, where the ground leveled off at the bottom of the hill, a large tent. A safe distance from the tent, a man squatted by a fire, stirring something in a kettle. A coffee pot sat in coals at the edge of the fire. A hundred yards or so away the mustangs grazed the nutritious mid-summer grass. A rider sat his horse, watching the herd.

"That's far enough," Adam said when they got to the bottom of the hill. Then he called, "Hey, Jerome! Help me get this kid tied up."

Jerome got up, went to the tent, and returned with a length of light rope. He tied Tommy's hands behind him, then bound his arms to a small tree. "That'll hold him," he grunted. The two men went to the fire.

Tommy shivered. The rain had stopped, but his clothes were still damp. He tested his bindings, and was not surprised to find that Jerome knew his ropes, and knots.

What have I done? Tommy asked himself. *My parents will never know what happened to me. Shadow and Little Bear may already be dead, already being eaten by scavengers. I won't get out of this mess. Adam is going to make sure of that.* Tommy recalled Steve's admonition, as they had parted that morning. "Don't get yourself shot," Steve had said.

Mexico Bill rode in. Without so much as a glance at Tommy, he went out to the herd of mustangs. The man who had been watching the horses rode back to the campsite. "What's for supper?" he inquired.

"Hi, Ramone," Jerome greeted the wrangler. "We'll have chili in a little while."

Ramone led his unsaddled horse a short way out, hobbled him, and came back to the campfire. "What's with the kid?" he asked.

"A snooper," Adam replied. "Same kid who found our cattle last fall, at the canyon. I'm gonna put a bullet in him and dump him down one of those old mine shafts."

"Him again?" Ramone shrugged. "I'm gonna take a nap. Wake me up when the chili's ready." He went to the tent and disappeared inside.

Tommy tried to move his feet and his hands to keep them from getting numb. His tightly bound arms ached. Had Steve gotten a message out, he wondered? *Yeah, he would find a way.* Tommy was certain of that. *But I don't think it will do me any good. Nobody will find me out here. Not in time to save me, anyway.*

He swallowed hard against the truth. He had blundered. This time there was no Shadow horse to save his hide, no helicopter winging in to protect him. The ropes would hold. His fate hung in the hands of outlaws.

It made him angry. Being tied to a tree, like an animal, made him angry. The fact that there were people to fear angered him. Most of all, he was angry at himself, ashamed of himself, really, for having been so careless.

As anger stirred him up, adrenalin shot through his veins. Tommy straightened up, looked at the two men by the fire, and thought, *I can outsmart those guys!*

Adam and Jerome were talking. Thinking he might hear something useful, Tommy tried to hear what they were saying. Adam said, "I know of an old cabin north of here. Maybe twenty miles. An old trapper's place, I think. Real wild country. A good place to hide, if worse comes to worse."

"That's good to know," Jerome replied. "We might have to change our plans." Were they worried, or was it just idle talk?

It's going to be dark soon, Tommy mused. *Been a long day. I haven't had anything to eat or drink since early this morning. Seeing that pot of chili doesn't help.* It didn't help, except that it gave him an idea.

It's a wild idea, Tommy thought. *A long shot. But I can't stand here feeling sorry for myself. I have to try to make something happen.*

"Hey, you guys!" he called. Both men looked up. "I feel kind of sick. I have to go, and I need a drink."

The mustangers looked at each other. Jerome shrugged. "Can't hurt nothin', I guess," he said.

"All right, but you keep your gun handy." Adam smirked, and added, "Be an awful shame if he tries something and we have to shoot him."

He went to Tommy, untied him from the tree, then untied his hands and re-tied them in front. *That's a break*, Tommy thought. Then he noticed Jerome at the fire, with his rifle in his hands, watching him closely. *Adam's setting me up. He wants me to make a run for it so he can shoot me. I wouldn't have a chance.*

Going down to the fire, Tommy pretended to be a little bit woozy. Standing by the fire, he trembled. Keyed up and nervous, it wasn't hard to do. He held out a shaking hand, asked in a pleading manner, "Can I have a sip of coffee?"

Adam bent over and reached for the coffee pot. *This is it!* Tommy's decision came in a flash, *It's now or never!*

With the speed and strength of desperation, Tommy took one step and kicked as hard as he could.

His aim was perfect. Adam pitched headfirst into the fire. He rolled away, cursing loudly.

Without losing a step, Tommy kicked his other booted foot through the fire, showering Jerome with blazing embers, glowing coals and hot ashes. Jerome screamed, covered his face with both hands and threw himself backward, moaning and swearing. Tommy leaped over the fallen man and ran for his life.

Two down and one to go! he exulted. He headed for the tent, kicked tent pegs out of the ground as he rushed past, and heard a startled and confused vaquero struggling to fight his way out from under the collapsed tent.

Without stopping to look back, Tommy fled into the woods, running as he had never run before. Behind him, he heard somebody yell, "Get him! Get him!" There was a gunshot.

14. TOMMY'S RUN

Tommy fought his way through the woods. He ducked low branches, dodged through underbrush and hurdled fallen trees. It was difficult with his hands tied. He continued his desperate flight for freedom until labored breathing and a pounding heart forced him to stop.

Gasping for breath, he listened. Angry shouting back at the camp had ceased. Then he heard somebody crashing through underbrush, swearing vehemently. Tommy grinned, thinking, *He won't keep that up for very long. Does he really think he can catch somebody that way?*

He walked quietly for a few minutes, then stopped. He raised his bound wrists to his face and gnawed at the knots with his teeth. Working patiently, he loosened the knots, and his hands were free. His wrists were rope-burned and sore, but he was free!

Tommy pocketed the rope; he would leave nothing to show where he had been, which way he was going. Boot prints in the rain-softened earth didn't matter. They couldn't track him in the dark. *By morning*, he hoped, *I'll be a long way from here. Maybe at Shepherds Lake. They'll guess that's where I'm going, will probably be watching for me. But I have to get there somehow.*

A breeze blew the clouds away, but there were no stars, no light at all. *I'll have to stick to this hillside, keep the uphill to my left. That way, I'll be going mostly east and north. That's the direction I have to go.*

It was slow going. Tommy went around impenetrable thickets, scrambled over or under storm-downed trees, or went around them. He tripped over hidden objects, stepped into holes, and thought he was never going to get anywhere. Then he reminded himself that every step counted, and that it was a whole lot better than being tied to a tree.

He struggled, hardly able to see where he was going, for about an hour. Then a few stars appeared, and soon a crescent moon came to help. And help it did! He made much better time, was even able to jog part of the time.

But he was tiring. He'd had nothing to eat or drink since early that morning. And his feet were getting sore. *Boots sure aren't made for running*, he mused. *I'm getting blisters. But they won't stop me. Bullets will. Bullets will stop me cold.*

Resigned to a night of painful toil, Tommy pushed on doggedly. He walked most of the time, climbed and crawled when he had to, jogged whenever he could. When he could see the north star, he dropped off the hill to flatter ground. With better light, more level terrain, and more open country, he made much better time.

But he needed a drink of water. Needed it badly. He had been sweating profusely, was approaching dehydration. He could fight everything but that. And so, when he came to a small stream, he didn't worry about beaver fever. He went to his knees and drank. He sat back, rested for a minute, then leaned down and drank some more. Not knowing when, or if, he would find water again, Tommy drank all the water he could hold.

Tommy reflected that his cross country running had prepared him well. He had learned the importance of water, had learned to pace himself, and had learned that he could continue to run long after he thought he couldn't run another step.

But how long could will power stave off fatigue? Would the night, and the nightmare, never end? *I have to rest,* he decided.

Tommy saw a log and sat down. His body slumped. The urge to lie down was overwhelming. It threatened to get the best of him. *Man*, he concluded, *if I sit here any longer, I'll fall asleep. I have to get up and get going*.

Just getting to his feet was an ordeal. And when he stood, the pain in his feet was all but unendurable. He stood wavering, thinking, *I'll never make it*. Then visions of Shadow, Little Bear, Mexico Bill and the mustangers flashed through his mind. Painful feet didn't matter; he had to make it.

Tommy took a step. Another. One more, and then he was walking. As it had done before, the pain subsided into a dull ache, something endurable, something he could block out.

Nevertheless, he was still tired, almost beyond endurance. Plodding, head down, he was going on automatic. But what was that? A bird, chirping? Was he hearing things? Tommy looked up, tripped over some small obstruction and nearly fell down. When he regained his balance, he looked up again. A small bird flitted away. And there was a light. A long way off. What, a cabin in the woods? A camper cooking his breakfast? Or was he hallucinating? Tommy stared, and a shiver went through him. "It's daylight," he exclaimed aloud. "It's morning. I'm gonna make it!"

The sun peeked over the horizon, and the sight gave Tommy a surge of energy. *It's like the cheering spectators at the finish line of a cross country run*, he thought. It gave a tired runner a shot of energy he didn't know he had.

Tommy strode on, and in his excitement nearly blundered out onto the trail. He caught himself in time, took a step back, looked both ways, and saw nobody.

He saw, only a few steps away, a grove of young spruce trees, six to eight feet tall. *That looks good*, he thought. *I'll hide in there and wait for somebody to come along. I'll be safer if I'm with other people.*

He crawled into the spruce grove and sat with his back against a tree, thinking, *Now all I have to do is sit here and watch. And I have to stay awake. I think I can do that.* But his determination exceeded his physical ability, and, without his knowledge, his eyes closed.

171

"Gotcha!"

Tommy's eyes snapped open. Adam stood, spraddle legged, in the trail, grinning maliciously. He spat a copious stream of tobacco juice and then, with exaggerated deliberation, brought his rifle to his shoulder.

It was just too much. Mexico Bill a traitor, Shadow and Little Bear doubtless dead, and he, too, was about to die. And he was too tired to care. He had done what he thought was right, had done his best, and still failed. He closed his eyes and waited for the bullet he knew was coming.

15. MEXICO BILL

Tommy flinched involuntarily when he heard the shot. But he felt nothing. Was death painless after all? But what was all the fuss? He heard scuffling, snarling, curses. Then a shout. "No! No! Stop it!"

He forced his eyes open. Swirling dust obscured what appeared to be a furious struggle. A man fought a snarling, snapping dog, tried to crawl away. Without thinking, Tommy called, "Little Bear!"

His voice was little more than a squeak, but the angry dog paused, turned his head, and hurled himself at Tommy.

Knocked over and nearly smothered by the ecstatic dog licking his face, Tommy decided that heaven was not at all as he had pictured it. Then he laughed. "I'm alive, Little Bear! We're both alive!"

He pushed Little Bear aside, sat up, and saw Mexico Bill standing in the trail with his rifle in his hands. Would the nightmare never end?

"Are you okay?" Bill asked.

Tommy felt waves of anger. "Am I okay? Yeah, sure, I'm having a picnic. Go ahead, finish your job!"

Bill held up a hand, and said, "Hold on, Tommy. I'm on your side. Trust me."

"But, I thought… You mean…"

"I know what you thought, but there was nothing I could do. I had to play my part, or we would both have been targets."

"You're not a mustanger?"

"No. I'm working for the BLM. I pretended to be a mustanger so I could find out who was doing the rustling and horse stealing. Had to get the evidence."

Bill handed him his rifle, and said, "Here, you watch Adam while I get my horse." Tommy grinned, reached into his pocket, and pulled out the piece of rope he had saved. He gave it to Bill, and said, "This belongs to Adam. I want to give it back."

Bill tied Adam's hands behind his back, and said, "Shoot him if you want to." He turned and walked up the trail. To get his horse. *But what about my horse*? Tommy wondered.

Bill reappeared, a long way away. With *two* horses! Could that be Shadow? Yes, there was no mistaking that proud stallion.

Shadow's alive! Tommy forgot he was tired, forgot his sore feet. He sprinted up the trail and grabbed Shadow's bridle reins. He put an arm over the mustang's neck, tried to hold back the tears. "Shadow," he said, quietly, "I thought I had lost you."

"Hey!" Bill called. "Let's get up to Shepherds Lake! Watch Adam while I get his horse."

Tommy hastily checked his cinch, stuck his foot in the stirrup and swung aboard. He sat for a minute, puffing, weak and shakey. *Man, I've had it. I'm worn out.* He had been going on nerve.

Bill brought Adam's horse out of the woods. He put the reins in Adam's hands, still tied behind his back, and said, "Here you go, Adam. We're going to let you walk. Tommy, lead the way."

Adam gave Mexico Bill a black look and shuffled sullenly up the trail.

16. BILL'S STORY

Campers at Shepherds Lake stared as an Indian youth on a proud bay stallion, a bound and battered man leading his horse, and a Mexican vaquero, riding a fine Quarter Horse, paraded silently through the camp. Bill showed his BLM I.D. and gave the campers a 'thumbs-up'.

"Let's go down to the end," he suggested. "We want to get away from the rest of the campers, and we need room for our horses."

At the last campsite, Bill dismounted and tied Adam to a tree. He turned to Tommy and said, "I'll take care of the horses. You take it easy." He handed Tommy his bedroll. Tommy unrolled it, sat down, and began pulling off his boots.

Bill unsaddled the three horses, led them down to a grassy area below the lake, and hobbled them.

"Want some coffee?" he asked, when he returned.

"Yeah, thanks. And give me my canteen. I need water. And can you bring me some lake water for my feet?"

"Sure thing," Bill replied. He handed the canteen and his thermos to Tommy, then went to the lake for wash water. When he saw Tommy's feet, he exclaimed, "Man, you need to see a doctor!"

"Soap and water will do it," Tommy replied. "And I have disinfectant salve in my first aid kit." Bill frowned, and started building a fire.

Tommy washed his feet, let them air dry, then applied salve and some stick-on patches, and, finally, he pulled on two pair of clean white socks. Then he looked at Bill, who was stirring something in a kettle, and said, "We wondered why you didn't show up in the valley this spring."

"The Bureau of Land Management asked me to help them find the outlaws who were rustling cattle and stealing wild horses. I decided the only way was to become a mustanger. I couldn't tell anybody what I was doing."

"That sounds like dangerous business."

"It's not something I want to do a whole lot of. I hope I don't ever have to do it again, for that matter. But sometimes we have to do things we don't like to do."

"And I came along and messed up your plan."

"It changed things when Adam found you. I had to try to figure out how to save your hide and continue to play my part. Hey, how about some potato soup?"

"Oh, boy! Yeah! By the way, how did Adam find me, yesterday?"

"An old stud kept looking up there, like he would if he saw another horse. Adam went to see, and I went up too. I didn't want some innocent person getting hurt. These guys are a bad lot."

"Tell me about it! Looks like I caused a lot of trouble. I owe you, big time."

"Who knows? Maybe it was a good thing. It speeded things up, that's for sure. We've got Adam, and the horses."

"How about the other two guys?"

"They ran off. I think they're headed for their hideout. How about another bowl of soup?" Tommy had emptied his bowl.

"Thanks. That really hit the spot. I think I dumped a whole kettle of chili last night, when I got away. Could have used some of that, coming through the woods."

"I'll bet. Well, get some rest. I have things to do."

Tommy drank the soup, stretched out on his bed, closed his eyes, and just got to sleep when Bill shook him.

"What's the matter?" he grumbled. "I just got to sleep."

Bill laughed, and said, "You've been asleep for two hours. Steve's here; I thought you might like to know."

Tommy sat up, and saw Steve, standing hip-deep in the lake, casting for trout.

17. THE POSSE

Tommy put on his old running shoes and limped out to the lake. "Hi, Steve!" he called. "How's fishing?"

Steve waded to shore, and said, "Fishing's good. Bill told me what happened. Hey, I thought I told you to be careful."

"Yeah. Well, I forgot. I messed up, big time. Did you contact the BLM or somebody?"

"Yes, I did. A camper at Lost Lake let me use his cell phone. I talked to a clerk at Rifle Gap. She said she was sure somebody would get up here as soon as possible today. Those cell phones are handy gadgets."

"Yeah, they are. Well, you catch some fish. I'll stir up the fire."

Tommy walked around, stretched, did some exercises to ease his sore muscles, and decided to make some coffee. He was squatting beside the fire when he heard the metal stock trailer coming on the dirt road. In another minute a BLM pickup truck pulled the trailer into the campground. Tommy waved, and the truck came to where he stood.

Deputy Sheriff John Hanson got out of the passenger side of the pickup, and smiled at Tommy. A tall, slender, weathered man slid out of the driver's side. Hanson introduced Tommy to Duane Blackstone. "Duane's in charge of the wild horse and burro program," Hanson explained. Then he asked, "Who's that, tied to the tree?"

"Adam Childers," Tommy replied. "He's one of the mustangers. And we have the horses."

"Really?" Blackstone's eyebrows shot up. "I have to hear about this! But let's unload our horses first." He went into the trailer and came out leading a stout bay mare. Then Hanson came out leading Old Faithful. He grinned, and said, "Here's an old friend of yours."

Tommy patted the tall horse, looked him over, and said, "He looks good. Real good."

"Yes, he's in good shape," Hanson agreed. Then he asked, "Where's Bill?"

"He's below the camp, where our saddle horses are pastured. You can take yours down there if you want to. They can get water, and there's plenty of grass."

When they had tended to their horses, they came back with Bill, and said, "Okay, Bill, fill us in."

Bill made it as short as possible. He finished by saying, "Two of the mustangers got away. I think I know where they're going."

Blackstone spread a map on the ground. Bill pointed. "See this old homestead? They've fixed it up some, use it for a hideout. We had planned to take the mustangs there, then get a trucker to come in on that old logging road and haul them out."

"I know about that old place," Blackstone said. "It's what, about thirty miles from here?"

"Not quite that far."

"Think we can catch them?"

"We might. But they have a good head start. And they have a pickup and horse trailer there."

"Maybe we need a chopper. What do you think, John?"

Hanson had been listening while he stirred pancake batter. He thought for a minute, then said, "I don't know. It might work. But if those guys see a chopper, they'll run, like they did at the canyon last fall. There's a lot of wild country out there."

"And we'll spend the rest of the summer trying to find them," Blackstone replied.

"We might try to catch them first," Hanson suggested. "Then, if we miss them, we'll call for the chopper. If they are using the pickup, they'll be easy to find from the air."

"That's a good idea. What do you think, Bill?"

"Yeah, that might work. Let's try it." Bill replied.

"Good," Blackstone said. "That's what we'll do. It's going to be a long ride. We'll travel as light as possible, won't eat again until we get back. How're the pancakes coming, John?"

"They're ready when you are." Steve had caught several rainbow trout to add to the pancakes, bacon and eggs, and coffee that John had prepared.

While they ate, Tommy said, "Bill, I worry about those horses that have a foot tied up. Can we do something about that?"

Bill smiled, and said, "Last night I persuaded Ramone to help me. We had no trouble roping them and cutting the ropes. He didn't much like that, either. They limped around for a while, but I think they'll be okay."

"Man, I 'm glad to hear that. It really bothered me," Tommy said.

The three men went to get their horses, and Tommy tried not to limp as he walked along to get Shadow. Blackstone said, "Tommy, there's no need for you to come."

"I want to go. I feel fine."

Then Deputy Hanson spoke up. "Tommy," he said, "we appreciate your offer. And we'd like to have you. But we can't allow someone your age to take part in a police chase. You and Steve stay here. We'll handle it."

"Okay, I understand," Tommy said. Then he smiled, and added, "I just think I have the best horse for a run like that."

"We can't argue with you on that score," Blackstone said. "You and Steve take care of things here. Get a few more rainbows if you can. We'll be hungry when we get back."

"And be careful around Adam," Bill cautioned. "He's a slick one."

"Right." Tommy replied. "Good luck." He watched the three men ride away, and thought, *Well, that's that. They know what they're doing. They can handle it*. He patted Little Bear on the head, and said, "We're okay now, Bear. Nothing to worry about any more." Little Bear wagged his tail.

Tommy went to his bed, wondering why he was uneasy. He lay down, and Little Bear curled up beside him. "I don't know why, Bear, but I feel like something's wrong. Like I'm forgetting something."

18. SHADOW'S RUN

Tommy lay awake. Something bothered him. But what? Mentally, he hashed over all that had happened since his capture. *Maybe I'm just too stuffed with food to sleep*, he thought, and smiled, remembering how hungry he was, only twenty four hours ago. And how that hunger triggered his escape. He pictured Adam and Jerome at the fire, talking.

"Adam and Jerome, talking! That's it!" he exclaimed. Little Bear leaped up in alarm, and Tommy laughed.

"Hey, Steve!" he called.

Steve left off washing the dishes and asked, "What's up?" Tommy pointed to his map, and said, "Look here. See this little trail going north?"

"I see it. What about it?"

"I overheard Adam telling Jerome about an old trapper's cabin, and a beaver pond, twenty miles north of here. Adam thought it would be a good place to go, a standby hideout 'in an emergency', is how he put it. I wondered at the time if they were beginning to mistrust Bill. I think, now that they know about him, they're on their way to this other place."

"And the posse is on a wild goose chase!"

"I think so. Wild country, Adam said. Those guys are on the run. See, here's the beaver pond, and the cabin. I'd forgotten all about that. Just now remembered."

"Now's when we need a cell phone."

"I have to go after those guys."

"Oh no, here we go again!" Tommy gave Steve a friendly punch on the arm, and said, "You'll have to stay here so you can tell the posse where I've gone." He hurried to the pasture to get Shadow.

"You're going just like that? No saddle? No boots?"

"I'm gonna ride Indian style."

"What next?" Steve muttered.

Tommy took the mecate from his saddle, wrapped it around Shadow's girth twice and tied it loosely. He jumped on, made some adjustments, and tied the knot tighter.

"There, now," he said, "my horse can go faster, and farther, than a horse carrying a heavy, tightly cinched saddle. And if it comes to a wild ride, I can shove my knees under the rope to help me stay on. And I can handle Shadow without a bridle. That frees both hands so I can use a gun, or whatever. Hand me Adam's carbine." He checked to make sure the gun was loaded, and Steve asked, "And you're going to ride all that way bareback?"

"Only way to go this time," Tommy replied. "Little Bear, I gonna ride too far, and go too fast, for you. You have to say here with Steve." Then, more sternly, "Bear, stay!" The forlorn dog sat, dejected, and watched Tommy ride away.

He went west, on the same trail the posse had taken. In about a mile, he found the little-used and partially hidden trail going north. He walked Shadow that first mile, and now let the eager horse jog. When Shadow began to sweat, Tommy pushed him to the slow lope that was easy on horse and rider.

He let Shadow lope for a couple of miles, then slowed him to a walk. But Shadow fretted; he wanted to go. "Well okay, if that's what you want to do," Tommy said. "Have your run. Take the edge off." He gave the stallion his head, and in a few strides was going at a strong gallop.

Tommy relished the ride, but after several miles he slowed the horse. And again, Shadow fussed, pulled on the bit. *Well*, Tommy thought, *he's breathing easy. And he's sweating lightly. He's just wasting energy dancing around. I might just as well let him go for a while.* He gave Shadow his head, and the strong horse immediately broke into the brisk gallop.

The ride was exhilarating. With the wind in his face, hair flying, branches whipping past, and the feel of the powerful horse under him, Tommy thought he knew how a warrior felt, in bygone years, pursuing an enemy, or chasing wild game. *But should I let him go like this? I don't want to ruin a good horse trying to catch worthless outlaws.*

Tommy looked at the horse. He noticed that Shadow was still sweating lightly. The sweat was clear, not lathering. And he was breathing easy, seemed to be running without effort. Suddenly Tommy thought, *He's running in rhythm. I've heard about this. His stride, his breathing and his heartbeat are all in rhythm. That's what marathon runners and endurance riders try to find. Shadow knows how do to that!*

If the ride was exciting, it was also distracting. How far had he come? How long had he been riding? Tommy didn't know. *I know we've made good time, though. I think I had better slow down before I run into somebody. All I really want to do is see if those two mustangers are up here.*

Tommy no more than thought that when Shadow raised his head and perked up his ears. He started to slow his horse, but it was too late. The rider Shadow had seen came into view. Ramone! Dragging his rifle from the scabbard!

It was too late for secrecy. Tommy dropped his knotted reins to let them hang over Shadow's neck, clutched the rifle with both hands, leaned forward and said, "Let's go, Shadow!"

The powerful stallion fairly leaped from the gallop into a breathtakingly fast run. Only his knees wedged under the girth rope kept Tommy on the charging horse.

Ramone twisted in his saddle, tried to get a one-handed shot off, and looked into the muzzle of Tommy's rifle. He fired a wild shot, then faced forward and spurred savagely.

"Don't make me shoot you, Ramone!" Tommy shouted. "Give me your gun!" Ramone held his rifle high, and Tommy grabbed it as he flew past. Fifty yards ahead, Jerome rode hard for the cabin.

Jerome looked back, saw Tommy coming fast, and thought, *The kid isn't even using his reins. He can't control that horse. I'll fool him.* As if trying to outrun Tommy, Jerome leaned forward, pretending to spur hard. Then, suddenly, he sat up, pulled back hard on his reins, and jumped off, calf roper style, as his horse slid to a stop. It was a good move, expertly executed.

Expecting to see the young Indian flying by on a runaway horse, Jerome turned and saw Tommy sitting his stopped horse, holding a rifle with both hands, and looking down the sights lined up squarely on him. "Drop it, Jerome!" Tommy's voice was harsh.

Jerome hesitated, glanced back up the trail, and dropped his gun seconds before a rawhide loop encircled Tommy's upper body. Tommy had not heard the running horse behind him.

Although Ramone had lost his rifle, he was not out of the fight, not while he still had his sixty-foot reata. His throw was good, but he had not anticipated Tommy's quick stop. Shadow lashed out with both hind feet at the overtaking horse, and Ramone, a dally man, had to drop his rope and grab his saddle horn as his horse shied violently. Without either his gun or reata, Ramone spurred furiously for the protection of the cabin.

Snap! Bang! Ramone heard the little sonic boom a split second before hearing the report of the rifle. The bullet had come close! He stopped, turned his horse around, and raised his hands in surrender.

Tommy caught movement out of the corner of his eye. Jerome was reaching for his gun. Tommy swung his rifle to cover the wiley outlaw and barked, "No, Jerome!" The mustanger froze. He had been too slow.

Tommy backed Shadow a few steps and called, "Get over here, Ramone!" The vaquero walked his horse closer. Tommy said, "That's good. Now re-set your saddles. Turn your pads over, and cinch up just tight enough to keep the saddles on while you lead your horse. I want to see you slide your hand under the cinch. That'll stop you from trying to mount and run off."

Three rifles, even the smaller carbines, were too many to carry. Tommy ejected the cartridges, left them lying where they fell, and tossed the unloaded guns to the men. "Put those in your scabbards," he ordered.

"Now, Ramone, start leading your horse up the trail. Jerome, you follow Ramone. And remember, I don't want to shoot you, but I will if I have to. Let's go!"

So far, so good. But now what do I do? Tommy wondered. He hadn't planned on this. The sun was going down; could he handle the two mustangers in the dark? He wished he could tie them, but he dare not attempt to do that. Not all by himself.

If I keep them moving, don't let them stop, maybe they will get too tired to be trouble. Then

193

Tommy smiled wryly. *Not those guys. They'll never be too tired. I'm the one who's tired.*

Then Jerome complained, "My feet are killing me. I can't walk any farther."

"You're breaking my heart," Tommy replied. "I walked all night in boots. You can, too. See how you like it."

19. THE MUSTANGERS ESCAPE

Won't that moon ever come up? Tommy wondered. He could barely see his captives. *Those guys know I can't see any better than they can. I have to keep them moving, let them know I'm still running the show.*

They came to a little stream that Tommy remembered. Shadow had leaped over it without slackening his pace. "All right," he called, "get yourselves a drink, and water your horses. One at a time. Ramone first."

Without comment, the mustangers took their turns, then resumed their march on the back trail. Tommy let Shadow drink, but he dare not get down for his own drink. *They're watching, every step of the way, just waiting for a chance to turn on me, or to run off.* Tommy knew better than to underestimate the toughness, and the capabilities, of the two men.

He thought it was close to midnight when the moon finally showed. It was just a waning crescent moon, but it gave welcome light. *Four or five hours till daylight. Can I stay awake that long? Man, I wish Steve was here.*

Tommy swung his arms, took deep breaths and pinched himself, trying to stay alert. In spite of everything, he caught himself nodding. *I wish I could get down and walk,* he thought. *But then I couldn't see those men at all.*

He rode on doggedly, half asleep in spite of efforts to remain alert, and was startled when Shadow abruptly stopped. His head was turned, ears pointing off to the left, as though watching something in the underbrush. There was a shadowy movement, and Jerome jumped out, brandishing his unloaded rifle like a club.

Shadow reared to strike at the attacking man. Jerome ducked and took a wild swing at Tommy. The gunstock hit him in the shoulder, glanced off and grazed his head.

Tommy slipped off his horse and landed on his back. He lifted his feet to deflect a blow, and rolled over. Before he could get up, he heard a shout, took a paralyzing hit on his back, and blacked out.

Somebody was shaking him, and Tommy tried to fight him off.

"Tommy! It's me, Steve!" Tommy stopped fighting and opened his eyes. "Steve!" he exclaimed. "How did you get here?" He tried to sit up, and Steve pushed him down.

"Hey, take it easy," Steve cautioned. "You might be bad hurt." Tommy lay back down, and Steve explained, "I got to worrying, and came out to find you."

"Where are Jerome and Ramone?"

"They're gone. When I rode up, I heard some commotion, but couldn't tell what was happening. I yelled, and I guess the mustangers thought I had a gun, or that there were more people. They grabbed their horses and ran."

Tommy sat up and said, "I think I'm okay. I've got a headache, and a sore back. Did you bring a canteen? I'm really thirsty."

"Yes, I'll get it." Steve left and came back with the canteen. Tommy took a long drink, looked around, and asked, "Where's Shadow?"

"They took him."

"Did you see which way they went?"

"West, through the woods. They'll be easy to track, but I guess we'll have to wait for daylight."

"Yeah, I suppose so." Tommy got to his feet and walked around to limber up his back, and then he said, "Listen. Maybe we don't have to wait."

They heard violent thrashing in the underbrush. Somebody hollered "Whoa! Whoa!" Then loud profanity, and the sound of a running horse. Tommy picked up his carbine, made sure it was loaded, and said, "Come on!"

They made their way through the woods as quietly as possible. In a small clearing they found Ramone, kneeling beside Jerome, who lay on his back, moaning. "Get up, Ramone!" Tommy barked.

Ramone looked up, startled. He raised his hands, stood up, and said, "Jerome's bad hurt."

"Well, I'm not a doctor. Steve, get some rope and tie Ramone to a tree. We'll tie Jerome's hands behind him, and tie his feet together, just in case. You watch these guys; I'm going to try to find Shadow."

He didn't have to go very far. He called to the horse as he walked, and in a few minutes he saw the stallion, standing head and ears up, waiting. Jerome's saddle hung under Shadow's belly, stirrups dragging on the ground.

"Hello, Shadow," Tommy said. He stroked the mustang's sleek neck, and said, "It's a good thing I got you used to having a saddle hanging that way. Stand still for a minute while I put it back where it belongs." He'd seen horses run off and kick a saddle to pieces when it turned under like that.

He led Shadow back to where Steve waited. "Still alive, are you Jerome?" he asked. "I'll saddle your horse. We're going to Shepherds Lake."

"I can't ride. I need help."

"Okay, you can stay here. I'll tie you to a tree, so you don't get lost. We'll be back some time tomorrow." Sputtering, moaning and groaning, Jerome got up and limped to his horse.

They created another stir when they rode into the campground. Two rough looking men, tied to their saddles, and two boys escorting them was not a common sight in a campground.

Duane Blackstone stared, open-mouthed. "Unbelievable!" was all he could think to say.

Mexico Bill chuckled, and said, "Those two boys've showed us up. I think there's a good story here."

"You can bet on it," John Hanson replied.

20. AT SHEPHERDS LAKE

"How come everything tastes so good outdoors?" Blackstone asked. The posse, with Tommy and Steve, sat at a campground picnic table.

"Fresh air, exercise, and a wood fire," Hanson suggested.

"Yeah, but eating only once a day might have something to do with it," Mexico Bill quipped. "But let's give John some credit. He's a real good cook."

"Amen to that. And rainbow trout out of that cold water can't be beat," Blackstone said. Then he asked, "Tommy, what made you decide to go up that trail?"

Tommy explained about hearing the two mustangers discussing an alternate escape plan. "I forgot about it until after you were gone. Then I thought, if they know Bill is a BLM man, they'll go to that other place."

"You rode hard to catch them. You said you have the best horse, and I guess you proved it. But why did you ride all that way bareback?"

Tommy explained, and said, "There's an old saying: A white man will ride a horse to exhaustion, or to death, but a Comanche will ride a horse to where he wants to go."

Hanson nodded, and said, "Yes, I've heard that. Some people claim the Comanches were the best horsemen in the world. How did you learn so much about that, Tommy?"

"From my grandfather; and I've read about it. They say that, although the Utes and Comanches were enemies, sometimes they rode together under a truce. On a big hunt, or against a mutual enemy. They found out that those who rode the best horses were the most successful. Comanches all rode. Men, women and children. They made up games to perfect their skills and test their horses."

"Were they the first to use the girth rope?" Blackstone asked.

"I don't know, but it's generally thought so. It helped them stay on their horses, and left both hands free for using a bow, or a lance, or whatever. And they learned how to control their horse without a bridle."

"That's pretty interesting," Blackstone said.

"Yes it is. The Comanches always used four wraps for their girth rope. The number four had spiritual significance. The four seasons, four directions, four-legged animals, things like that."

"They had a reason for everything. Tommy, your mecate is beautiful. I'll bet it's hand made."

"Yes. Frank Lucero, they call him Lucky, made it for me. He's an inmate at the Canon City prison. He's a rawhider and a braider. He saw me on TV, when I went to the Fort Worth rodeo to get Shadow back after he'd been stolen. I did my little 'Indian' act, and Lucky liked that. He said he got mane and tail hair from inmates who worked with the mustangs being prepared for adoption. Sent it to me for Christmas."

"It's special, all right. Something to be proud of." Hanson turned to Blackstone, and said, "Duane, that reminds me. What will happen to the mustangers' horses and other possessions if they're convicted?"

"The court decides that, if they don't have relatives to take care of personal property. Bill, do you know if those men have families?"

"Ramone might. The other two are drifters."

"I'm thinking there might be somebody who would keep the horses for the use of them," Hanson said. "I'm kind of re-hab minded, and think those men would make good ranch hands if they will go straight when they get out."

"Yes, and it might be an incentive for them. Do you have anybody in mind?"

"No. It just occurred to me. But I'll ask around."

"All right, see what you can do. But the court will have to approve."

"I'll get on it. By the way, is somebody coming to pick up our prisoners?"

"There's a van on the way. And they're bringing a man to drive my rig back. We'll have to drive the mustangs to Rifle Gap Park."

Tommy looked up asked, "Could we help you do that?"

"You've already done more than your share. And you came here to fish, remember?"

"We just wanted a trip. Fishing was only a part of it. What do you say, Steve?"

"Sure, I'd like to do that. We have to be getting back in a day or so anyway."

"Okay, if you're sure," Blackstone replied. "But we won't leave until tomorrow. You still have time to fish."

"And sleep," Tommy sighed. "But first I want to say goodbye to our friends."

He walked to where the captives sat in their "tree" jail and said, "If you get sent to Canon City, and happen to meet Frank Lucero, tell him 'hello' for me. Tell him I really like my mecate, and I'm making good use of it."

Adam and Jerome scowled, but Ramone nodded. And that winter Tommy got a Christmas card from Lucky, with a note saying that he and Ramone had become friends, and that Ramone never gets tired of talking about Tommy's Comanche ride.

EPILOGUE

When Tommy graduated from high school, he hoped some day to work for the Bureau Of Land Management, or the Forest Service. With that goal in mind, and following the advice of his parents and others whose opinions he respected, he enrolled at Colorado State University at Fort Collins.

A little homesick, and missing the wide open spaces, Tommy struggled at first. But he stuck to it, and in his second year found his courses more interesting. He made many new friends, ran both track and cross country, and knew he had made the right decision. He was surprised, too, to find that the more he learned, the more there was to learn.

But his enthusiasm went downhill when his mother called early one morning in April. Obviously upset, she said that somebody came during the night and cut the wire on the big corral. The horses were gone.

"Gone?" Tommy was shocked. "All of them? Shadow too?"

"All but Blackie. He was in the little corral behind the barn."

"Is Dad there? Did you call the sheriff?"

"Dad was away on Forest Service work, but he'll be home tonight. And yes, I called the sheriff. There's nothing to go on, really. He thinks it was just a random act of vandalism. No obvious motive. Almost impossible to find whoever did it."

"I'll come home right away. I think I can get a bus out of here this morning."

"No, Tommy! I don't think you should do that. You can't waste a whole semester's work. There's only a month left. And maybe the horses haven't gone very far. They might even come back for their evening feeding."

"Yeah, I guess you're right," Tommy agreed. But before hanging up, he said, "But Mom, don't blame yourself. It's not your fault."

But the horses didn't come home, and nobody reported having seen them. And so, the day after he got home from college, Tommy saddled Blackie and began his search. He had to find the shadow horse, and the mares that belonged to other ranchers.

When he could get time off from his own ranch work, Steve rode with Tommy. They prowled the mountain meadows, the canyons, the forrested slopes, all without success. Deep in unfamiliar territory, they stopped at a small stream, where they unsaddled, hobbled both Diamond Lil and Blackie, spread their saddle blankets in the sun to dry, and lay back to rest their saddle-weary bodies.

"Summer's almost over," Steve commented. "Are you going to go back to school this fall, or will you stay out here as long as the weather permits?"

"Man, I don't know." Tommy was glum.

"Well, if you decide to stay, I'll stay, too."

"No, you won't!" Tommy was serious. "I talked you into going to college, and you're gonna go! This is my problem. It's my responsibility, and I don't intend for it to mess up anybody else's plans." Steve knew better than to argue the point; Tommy always meant what he said.

Fall was in the air in the high country. Steve had left, the deer, elk and other wildlife were drifting down to lower elevations, and Tommy did the same. He camped beside a little creek, and left Blackie, hobbled, to graze and rest in a small clearing about a hundred yards downstream.

Tommy sat on his bootheels the next morning, tending his little cooking fire. He turned his bacon, then put the small trout he had just caught in the frying pan with the bacon. "Here you go, Bear," he said, and tossed a strip of venison jerky to the patiently waiting, and watching, dog. "I can't give you any of this greasy stuff. Now, go hunt. See what you can find. Go on!" As though waiting for just those words, the shaggy dog bounded off, tail waving, on the scent, real or imagined, of some wild creature.

What is there about Labor Day? Tommy wondered. He reflected that five years ago, almost to the day, he caught the wild stallion. Then, a couple of years later, also on a Labor Day weekend, he found a heard of stolen cattle and got himself shot for his trouble.

And here it is again, he mused. *It's Labor Day, and here I am, in the middle of nowhere, trying to find the shadow horse. It's getting spooky.*

So, Tommy, what are you going to do now? He asked himself. Common sense said he should give up the fruitless search, go home, and get back to Colorado State for the beginning of the fall semester. But his heart said otherwise. He knew that, if he failed to find the stallion, riders would be carrying rifles, and they would have orders to shoot the horse on sight. And if that didn't work, then ranchers would, in all probability, use an airplane, or a helicopter, to find the horse. And when they found him, they would run him to exhaustion and riddle him with bullets. Tommy shuddered at the thought.

"With his heart on the ground," as his grandfather would say, he shuffled down to the creek, where he scoured his frying pan, knife, and fork with sand, rinsed them and put them on a flat rock to dry. Then, lost in thought, he sat, his back against a tree in the warming sun.

Without even thinking about it, Tommy fished his flute out of his pocket and then, for the next few minutes, the plaintive call of the mourning dove echoed through the valley, to lose itself in the mountain wilderness. Though it was the wrong time of the year to hear a dove, the beautiful, haunting song was special to Tommy; if the shadow horse heard it, he would know it was Tommy calling.

He shoved his flute back in his pocket, started to get up, then froze. Something was watching him. How he knew, he could not say, but he knew. He always knew. Trusting his instincts, he stood up, very, very slowly. Any sudden movement would frighten a wild animal, might even provoke and attack.

Then he heard it, that soft nicker, no more than a flutter of the nostrils. Shadow's gentle greeting!

Almost afraid to believe his eyes, Tommy looked and there, not ten yards away, Shadow stood calmly, tossing his head.

On shaking legs, still hoping it was not a dream, he walked to the waiting horse. He put his hand on the velvety neck, and whispered, "Shadow, I couldn't find you, but you found me." It was all he could manage to say.

Impulsively, Tommy gathered a handful of mane and swung to the stallion's sleek back.

And then, if the ghosts of Indians, trappers or others who roamed those mountains in bygone years still kept watch, they well might wonder, certainly would marvel, at the curious sight of a slender young Indian, astride a beautiful Mustang stallion, cantering briskly, but unhurridly, this way, that way and every which way through the trees, floating, like smoke, through the forest.

There was nothing curious about it, actually. It was just Tommy Lewis and the shadow horse, playing.

Carl Mapps

The author on his Arabian stallion, on whom he won a hundred mile competitive endurance ride.

A veteran of World War II, Mapps took basic training at Fort Riley, Kansas, with horses. After serving for a short time in the U.S. Army Remount, he went overseas with the First Cavalry Division.

After the war, Mapps graduated from the College of Agriculture, University of Wisconsin. He then worked as ranch manager and horse trainer on several ranches. He says that all of his stories, though fiction, are realistic. Locals, events and horse handling methods are authentically portrayed.

Now retired, he lives in his home town of Green Lake, Wisconsin. Mapps says he reads a lot, writes a lot, goes fishing occasionally, and soaps his saddle once a year, whether it needs it or not.

Printed in the United States
53122LVS00001B/196-279